Hawaii Magic

"I've never done anything like this before... I mean with someone I barely know."

A small smile crept free. "Just think of it as part of the adventure." He reached up and traced a finger over her lips. She felt herself shaking.

"If this isn't what you want, just say so," he whispered. "Yes, I'll be disappointed, but I'd never force you into something you don't want to do."

He bent and slid a kiss over her earlobe. "But know this, if it is what you want, I plan to make love to you in every room of this house. Outside, too."

Fiji Fantasy

"So, what is your role?"

She smiled again, and Michael realized he could really get addicted to those smiles. "Actually, I was wondering the same thing about you." She took a sip of her drink and very deliberately set it down before reaching over to place her small hand on his thigh. "Are you a dream fulfiller, Michael?"

He caught himself just before his eyes drifted down to her cleavage, which was swelling over the top of her dress ever so nicely. "Depends on the dream."

"Well..." Her hand slowly inched up his thigh, and Michael steeled himself against the urge to pick her up, sling her over his shoulder and carry her out of the place. What was it about this woman that gave him such crazy thoughts?

"I had this dream of having one wildly passionate night with a stranger."

Books by Beverly Jenkins

Kimani Romance

Rhythms of Love with Elaine Overton
Baby, Let It Snow with Elaine Overton
Island for Two with Elaine Overton

BEVERLY JENKINS

has received numerous awards for her works, including two Career Achievement Awards from *RT Book Reviews* magazine and a Golden Pen Award from the Black Writer's Guild. She has also been featured in many national publications, including the *Wall Street Journal, People, Dallas Morning News* and *Vibe.* She has lectured at such prestigious universities as Oberlin University, the University of Illinois and Princeton. She speaks widely on both romance and nineteenth-century African-American history. Visit her website at www.beverlyjenkins.net.

* * * * *

Books by Elaine Overton

Kimani Romance

Fever
Daring Devotion
His Holiday Bride
Seducing the Matchmaker
Sugar Rush
His Perfect Match
Miami Attraction
Rhythms of Love with Beverly Jenkins
Baby, Let It Snow with Beverly Jenkins
Island for Two with Beverly Jenkins

ELAINE OVERTON

currently resides in the Detroit area. She has written twelve books and anthologies for BET Books and Kimani Press. She is an administrative assistant, currently working in the automotive industry.

Island
For Two

BEVERLY JENKINS
ELAINE OVERTON

KIMANI™
ROMANCE

 **KIMANI PRESS™**

ISBN-13: 978-0-373-86261-0

ISLAND FOR TWO

Copyright © 2012 by Harlequin Books S.A.

The publisher acknowledges the copyright holders of the individual works as follows:

HAWAII MAGIC
Copyright © 2012 by Beverly Jenkins

FIJI FANTASY
Copyright © 2012 by Elaine Overton

Recycling programs for this product may not exist in your area.

www.kimanipress.com

Printed in U.S.A.

Dear Reader,

After writing this book, I'm placing the beautiful island of Kauai on my bucket list. I knew next to nothing about Hawaii's other islands until I began my research, and once I learned there were filmed helicopter tours of Kauai online, I grabbed a seat, strapped myself in and went flying. *Wow,* is about all one can say about the breathtaking scenery.

If you'd like to experience the helicopter tour our hero, pilot Steve Blair, gives our heroine, Anita Hunt, go online, search for helicopter tours in Kauai and prepare to be mesmerized. I'm betting you'll place Kauai on your bucket list, too.

Beverly

CONTENTS

HAWAII MAGIC

Beverly Jenkins

Chapter 1

Lawyer Anita Hunt scrolled through the lengthy legal document on her laptop searching for typos and wording mistakes. She was so tired it was difficult to tell what was written correctly and what wasn't, but the contract was due to be presented to the parties involved in a few days so it had to get done. The document pertained to the Bentley file, a merger between two of the largest banks in Orange County, and for the past six weeks, she'd been burning the candle at both ends in an effort to tie it up. The project was a big one and, if she did well, she hoped her firm, Sheridan Law, would reward her with the partner status she'd been working so hard to attain.

Confident she'd dotted all her *i*'s and crossed all her *t*'s she took one last look at the final agreement's signatory page, and clicked Save. While the computer did its thing, she sighed wearily. *Goodness, I'll be glad when this is done.* She couldn't remember the last time she had gotten a full night's sleep.

Her boss, firm founder, Jane Sheridan, stuck her graying

blond head in the open doorway. "I thought you'd be gone by now, Anita."

A confused Anita paused. "Gone?"

"Your fiancé?" Jane replied, eyebrow raised.

"Oh, damn! Greg!"

Jumping to her feet, she quickly powered off the computer, stuffed it into its leather carrier and grabbed her handbag. Greg had flown in earlier in the day from D.C. specifically to see her on his way to Tokyo, and she'd been so deep into the merger documents, she'd forgotten their dinner date. "Jane, I know I promised you'd have this in the morning—"

"Don't worry about that. Just go. I can't believe you forgot."

The chagrined Anita couldn't, either. "I'll see you tomorrow."

Anita hurried past her on her way to exit the building.

In her car, Anita peeled out of the garage and headed for the freeway. She felt terrible. Getting across L.A. quickly at this time of the day was going to be next to impossible. Sending up a prayer to the Traffic Gods for grace, she hit the sync on the dash tied to her phone. "Hey, honey."

Greg's voice came on. "Where are you?"

"Caught in traffic," she lied. "Be there in about twenty minutes."

"Okay. Drive safely."

She sighed. He was such a gem.

She made it to Zola's Restaurant in record time. Wrangling a reservation on half-a-day's notice from such a premier establishment would've been impossible had she not known the Zola family, but luckily her father first introduced her to Mr. Zola and his fine food back when she was a teen.

Turning her car over to the valet, she hurried inside. Hector Zola, the owner, met her at the maître d' station. "Good evening, Anita."

"Hi, Uncle Hector. I'm sorry I'm late."

"No problem. We're taking real good care of him. This way, please."

"Thank you," she gushed.

"Sorry I'm late," she said again, this time to Greg. She gave him a quick peck on the cheek before settling into the chair Mr. Zola held out for her on the opposite side of the table. Greg didn't care for public displays of affection and neither did she. She offered Mr. Zola a silent thank-you and he withdrew soundlessly.

As always, Greg was impeccably dressed. Expensive suit and tie, and handsome enough to draw the discreet interest of some of the women seated around the dining room.

"It's good to see you," he said to her. The genuine pleasure he radiated melted her guilt-filled stress.

"Good to see you, too, and thanks for the surprise."

"When the travel office offered me the choice of flying out of Washington or L.A.—no-brainer. Glad it worked out. Been missing you."

"Same here." He was so sweet.

"Any word on making partner yet?" he asked.

"No." She took a small sip from her water—Perrier, ice and a twist of lemon.

"You should consider looking at other firms, Anita."

"I like where I am."

"You should be partner by now." He picked up his linen napkin and placed it on his lap.

"Maybe, but I'm going to hang with Sheridan for now."

His features showed he didn't agree with the strategy but he didn't press. They'd had this discussion before. Greg was a topflight lawyer for the Justice Department, and he'd made it clear that he wanted his future wife to be just as prestigious. She wanted to please him but lately, and she had no idea why, the more status she acquired for herself within Sheridan Law, the less comfortable fitting into his box became.

Hector sent over one of the waiters, and their conversation paused in order to give the young woman their orders.

After her departure, Anita relayed nonchalantly, "My mother wants to know when we're setting the date for the wedding. She's getting pretty antsy."

Pushy was more the word. Her mother, Circuit Court Judge Diane Whitehall Hunt, considered Greg a perfect example of what a son-in-law should be. Harvard Law, financially sound, up-and-coming career. He was steady, honorable and the son of one of her dearest sorority sisters. Both mothers were ecstatic at the idea of uniting the families.

His phone sounded. "Hold on a minute." He lowered his eyes to the display. "It's a text from Marie. She's the other lawyer going to Tokyo...."

As his thumbs worked the keypad, she saw him smile. Anita knew how busy he was, hell, she was busy, too, but a part of her resented the interruption.

"Okay. I'm done." He set aside the phone. "You were saying?"

"The wedding."

"Aah. My mom's giving me flack, too, so how about we deal with it next week after I get back? That way we can check our calendars and see what's what."

"That's fine, so how are you?"

"Doing well."

"What's going on in Tokyo?"

"Bribery investigation. Heading there to interview a few people. Shouldn't be more than three or four days. You look tired," he added.

"I'm dead on my feet. I'm finishing up the Bentley merger and haven't been getting much sleep—strike that, any sleep."

"Why're you letting Sheridan work you to death?"

"Because I love the challenge. I love the pace. I love the no sleep, too, most of the time. This is the firm I want to be a part of, and if I slack off, somebody else's name will be on the partner list."

He shook his head as if still not agreeing. "You could make twice the money somewhere else."

She raised her water glass in agreement. "True, but it's not always about the money." Sheridan Law specialized in corporate mergers. It was a small firm but so well respected it could afford to pick and choose its clients. The staff was predominantly female and, although Jane Sheridan was a demanding boss, she was fair, treated everyone equally and never took credit for the work done by her associates.

Dinner arrived. He had the sirloin. She had what she always ordered at Hector's: the grilled chicken wrap and the baby spinach salad topped with the house vinaigrette.

While they ate, Greg did most of the talking. Nothing new there. They'd been together since her senior year in high school. Back then, and all through college, she hadn't minded deferring to him because she'd lacked the confidence to do otherwise and she loved him. Tonight though, as she listened to him to drone on about how this Tokyo investigation might help him move up in the department, she found herself contemplating spending the rest of her life sitting quietly and listening to him while her accomplishments played second fiddle. It came to her that she was being far more introspective and critical than usual. She chalked it up to being bone tired and set aside the disquieting thoughts. She loved Greg. He treated her well and would be a good provider for the two kids they both wanted down the line. As her mother constantly pointed out, a girl couldn't do much better than Greg Ford.

"Are you listening, babe?"

His voice brought her to the present. "Sorry. I was back at the office. What did I miss?"

"Me talking about having to go right to my hotel room after we're done here. That text from Marie was to let me know that the report we've been waiting on just downloaded and we need to review it before we take off in the morning."

"You can't review it on the ten-hour flight to Japan?"

"Too many confidential details. Discussing it on the plane won't work."

"I see. At least we did get to spend time with each other." Due to their crazy and always-full schedules, this was their first face-to-face in three months. Living on separate coasts didn't help, either. Once they married, everyone assumed she'd move East and she, during the early days of their relationship, had, as well. Now? Once again, she pushed the thoughts away because she was too tired to deal with the inner turmoil.

When they finished dinner, he paid the check and walked her to the door. Outside, the night air felt good after being cooped up in air-conditioning all day. She looked up at the sky. Stars rarely showed themselves in L.A. due to all the pollution and tonight was no exception.

While they waited for the valets to bring their vehicles, he gave her a quick kiss. "Been great seeing you. Sorry I can't stay longer."

"Me, too, but it's okay. We both love our work." His having to rush off meant no intimate interlude, either; not that she cared that much for sex, but it might've been nice to share some quiet time together afterward. "Text me, when you get to Tokyo."

His car arrived. "I will. Try and get some rest and think about changing firms, okay? Somewhere near Washington."

She didn't reply to that. "Be safe," she called back instead.

He gave her a wave and drove off. That he hadn't waited around, to make sure she got into her own car safely, made her sigh.

"A gentlemen never leaves his lady standing alone on the curb."

Smiling, she turned to see Mr. Zola beside her. The disapproval on his face was plain.

"Are you standing in for Daddy tonight?" Her father was in Peru on a movie shoot with one of his marquee clients.

"I am. Just like he would stand in for me."

"I'm not upset with Greg for taking off," she lied. "He had work to do back at his hotel."

"No man who cares for you should be too busy to close you into your car."

Mr. Zola had five daughters and he was hell on the guys who came calling. Three of his daughters were now married, leaving the sixteen-year-old twins and their boyfriends as targets of his old-school parenting.

"You're making a big deal out of nothing, Uncle Hector."

He kept further comments to himself.

Her car finally arrived. He escorted her around to the driver side, saying, "Now this is how it's done."

Chuckling, she got in. "Thank you."

"Drive safely."

"I will."

He closed the door and she drove away.

A weary Anita trudged zombielike through the door of her condo and dropped her bag onto the sofa. The small reserve of energy she'd conjured up in order to be with Greg was gone. Her body screamed for sleep but she walked into her small home office and booted up her laptop instead. Her disquiet over Greg continued to play in the back of her tired mind and, for a moment, she allowed herself to admit she'd been feeling out of sorts with the relationship for some time. She liked her job and wanted to make partner. Marrying Greg meant she'd have to give that up and she thought enough of herself and her abilities to find that problematic.

She sat on her office sofa and removed her pumps. Weariness washed over her like the Pacific hitting the rocks at Malibu and she rested her head on the sofa's back. Her plan was to close her eyes for just a moment, then start on the Bentley file, but as soon as her lids lowered, she was asleep.

Chapter 2

In the dream, Anita was running frantically through a house with glass walls trying to find a phone that was ringing. She went from room to room searching high and low but the phone was nowhere to be found. As it kept chiming, she sensed herself waking up and realized the sound was coming from her own phone. She reached for it blindly. "Hello," she said into it groggily.

"Are you okay?"

Confused, Anita ran a hand over her face. "Jane?"

"Yes. You missed the staff meeting. Just trying to make sure nothing's wrong."

Instantly awake and alert, Anita sat up. "Oh, Lord! What time is it?"

"Ten."

"Oh, God!" A hasty look around the surroundings showed her in her home office on the sofa and dressed in the blue suit she'd worn yesterday. "Oh, Jane. I am so sorry—I overslept."

"Quite all right. Are you coming in?"

"Yes, I am." She was suddenly petrified.

"Think you can make it by, say, noon?"

"Yes. If not sooner."

"Good. Come see me before you go to your office, okay?"

"Yes, ma'am."

The call ended and Anita fell back onto the sofa. Her career was over!

She quickly showered, dressed herself in a black power suit and applied her makeup. If she was going to be fired, she'd at least look good cleaning out her office. Kicking herself for falling asleep and setting this nightmare in motion, she checked one last time in the mirror and headed out the door.

Jane's assistant, Val George, glanced up from her desk when Anita walked into the outer office. "Not like you to miss a meeting." Val was a law school student at UCLA who spent her lunch hours buried in a romance novel. "We were worried something bad had happened."

"Sorry. Is she ready for me?" Anita dearly wanted to ask Val's opinion on why Jane requested to see her first thing, but held her tongue. She'd know soon enough.

"She's ready. Go on in."

Head held high, Anita went through the door into the founder's inner sanctum.

"Good afternoon, Anita. Have a seat."

Anita complied and pulled in a deep breath to steady herself. "I'd like to apologize for missing the meeting this morning."

Jane waved her off. "We've all missed something due to lack of sleep. I overslept my very first day in court. Thought for sure the managing partner would fire me."

"But he didn't."

"Oh, yes, he did, and out of that grew Sheridan Law."

It was Anita's first time hearing how the firm began.

"You've been doing a superb job on the Bentley merger."

"Thank you."

Jane's affectionate smile did nothing to diminish Anita's embarrassment. You don't make partner oversleeping.

"In fact, you've done so well, I'm considering you for partner."

Her jaw dropped. Although she'd been wanting the partnership, hearing that she was nearly there left her rocked.

"Not like you to be speechless, Anita."

"Not like you gave me a clue to this."

Jane laughed.

Anita relaxed a bit. They got along well, but Jane didn't get along well with lawyers on the other side. What they called her often rhymed with *witch*.

"I'm considering you because you not only work hard, but you're fearless, as well. I've never had anyone stand up to me the way you did with that Foreman debacle last year."

Anita had been the only one at the firm to think it a bad idea to partner financially with Foreman Investment in its bid to take over one of the failing Detroit automakers. Because Foreman's CEO, Betsy Foreman, and Jane were sorority sisters, everyone involved considered Sheridan's role to be a no-brainer, but Anita hadn't been convinced that it was in the firm's best interest to do so—especially not financially. To Jane's credit, she let Anita present her case, and when Anita finished breaking down the facts and figures, and threw in the detail that no one at Foreman knew anything about automobile manufacturing, Jane grudgingly but wholeheartedly agreed.

"I'm honored by your faith in me, Jane."

"It's a faith you've earned."

Outwardly, Anita was a study of sedate calm. Inside however, she was jumping up and down like a kid at Christmas.

"I do have one concern, though."

The party screeched to a halt. "And that is?"

"When was the last time you took time off?"

"When I came down with mono last year." The work on that same Foreman issue left Anita so mentally and physically drained, she'd come down with mono and had to be hospitalized for a few days.

"But no time off for yourself." It was a statement, not a question.

"I'd rather work. I've wanted to be a lawyer since I was eight years old. Both my parents are lawyers. My work is my life."

"I'm not trying offend you, but you need more balance if you want to be a partner here."

"But you just stated you liked my hard work."

"I do, but I don't want to make you a partner only to have you drop from exhaustion every time we catch a case. I need you to learn to step away now and again."

Anita kept her face neutral. "So what do you recommend?"

"Ten days off—"

"But—"

"In Hawaii. It's one of the most beautiful places on the planet and it'll offer you a chance to get some rest and recharge your batteries. Beneath all that glam of yours, you're exhausted and, whether you admit it or not, it shows."

Anita wanted to argue. The Bentley case still had a ton of small details needing to be nailed down and since she'd ridden point, she was supposed to handle them. She couldn't do that if she was in freaking Hawaii, but the determination in Jane's eyes let her know that the Boss Lady wouldn't be moved by anything Anita had to say, so she sighed instead.

Jane's small smile showed her approval of the silent surrender. "Thanks for not turning this into a knock-down, dragout argument. If it'll make you feel better, the firm will be footing the bill as part of the bonus you've earned for the Bentley matter."

It didn't.

"I'll also be giving you an agenda, because I want to make certain you enjoy yourself."

Anita stared in disbelief.

But Jane didn't seem bothered by that, either. Instead, she said, "Val has all your travel documents, so check with her."

"And when am I leaving?" Anita asked.

"The day after tomorrow so get what you need from your office and go home and get some sleep. I don't want to see you back here until you return from vacation."

Tight-lipped, Anita stood. "Thank you."

Jane nodded.

Back in her own office, Anita plopped down angrily in her leather chair. She didn't like being ordered to do this, even though a little voice inside agreed with Jane's assessment by pointing out that the only life Anita had outside of her Black-Berry was her long-distance relationship with Greg.

She stood and walked over to the window of her high-rise office and looked down on the sprawling city that had become her home. She loved L.A.—the hustle, the bustle, the crowds. What in the hell was she going to do in Hawaii?

On the drive home, Anita's happiness over the news from Jane was tempered by the directive to go to Hawaii, but deciding to embrace the happy part, she called her mother. Anita was born in New York. Her parents divorced when she was young. Her mother, Diane, retained custody but Anita spent her summers with her entertainment lawyer dad, Randall, in California where he had moved after the split. Loving him was easy because he was so carefree and open, but loving her controlling, sharp-tongued mother was work.

The call went through to Diane's clerk, a man named Basil Watts. "Morning, Basil. Is the judge available?"

"Hi there, Anita. Hold on. I'll see."

Anita didn't know what her mom's schedule for the day might be, but hoped she wasn't in the middle of court. For

Diane, work trumped everything. Anita was accustomed to her mother's devotion to her work and when she was young, she'd always longed to rank higher on her mom's to-do list. However, as she grew older, she realized that would never be.

A second later her mother was on the line. "Anita. How are you?"

"Fine, Mother. You?"

"On my way to the bench, so this call has to be quick. How's Greg? Sylvia said he'd be stopping in to see you on his way to Tokyo." Sylvia was Greg's mother.

"He did, but he was so busy we didn't have time for more than a quick dinner."

"Have you set a date yet?"

Anita shook her head at her mother's single-mindedness. "No, but we'll do it when he gets back."

"Good. Anything else?"

She could see her mother consulting her watch. "Jane told me this morning that she's considering me for partner."

"Considering? Not recommending? You know those are two different things, don't you, Anita?"

"I do, Mother."

"Well, let me know when the latter precedes the former. For the record, I agree with Greg. You should be considering a firm here on the East Coast."

So much for my good news, Anita thought to herself. "Okay, Mother, I'll let you get back to your duties. Just keeping you in the loop."

"Set the date for the wedding just as soon as Greg returns. We'll talk then."

End of call.

Later, Anita got a much better reaction from her father in Peru via Skype. He was one of the top entertainment lawyers in the business. When she told him, his face lit up the screen.

"A consideration is just a few inches from recommendation, baby girl. So proud of you. Wow! When did this happen?"

"Today. Jane said she loves my work and my fearlessness."

A smile creased his handsome face—he was known for his good looks, as well. "Congratulations. Were I there, we'd be breaking out the champagne."

"Thanks, Daddy." He was her most favorite person in the world, bar none.

"You call your mother?"

"Yes. She said to let her know when Jane recommends me for partner as opposed to considering me."

He sighed audibly. "Good old Diane. You can always count on her to ruin the party."

"Dad," she said warningly.

"Sorry."

The small smile playing across his lips showed he wasn't really, but it was okay. She loved them both and was accustomed to their snipping at each other.

"Did you call Greg?"

"He's in Tokyo. I sent him a text but no reply yet." She filled in her father on their short dinner date last evening. "He still wants me to move back East. Said I should be partner with Sheridan by now."

"And what did you say?"

"That I'll stick with Jane presently."

"Good girl." Unlike her mother, her father had his misgivings about his only child marrying Greg, but he loved Anita enough not to make an issue of it. Most of the time.

Anita said gloomily, "Oh, and Anita's making me go to Hawaii."

"Why the long face?"

"Because it's a vacation."

He laughed.

She smiled. "What's so funny?"

"You, sweetheart. You look and sound so much like your mother."

"I'm going to take that as a compliment you know."

"And you should, but Hawaii's beautiful."

"But I have work to do here." She explained the Bentley case to him and about the final issues still needing to be handled.

"Did Jane say why she wanted you to go on vacation?"

"Said she needs me to stop and take a breath every now and then. I think it's because of the mono I caught last year."

"I'll be wiring her the biggest bouquet of roses I can find."

Her eyes widened with alarm. "Why?"

"For making you take time off."

She sat back against her chair, folded her arms and pouted mockingly. "I knew you'd take her side."

He chuckled. "And you were right." He studied her silently for a moment. "I know you love your work, Anita—you get that from your parents and there's nothing wrong with it. However—"

"However?"

"I need you to tap into both your gene pools, not just your mother's."

"Meaning I should run around with actresses, go to all-night parties and be a jet-setter like you?"

He dropped his head. "Touché. No, but I do want you to put some fun in your life, girl. You can't take your BlackBerry with you to the other side. Let go sometimes."

"But I do," she replied coming to her own defense, even though they both knew she was lying like a kid busted with a hand in the cookie jar.

He laughed again. "Oh, really? When was this?"

"Greg and I went to Cancun two years ago."

"And how long did you stay?"

She looked down at her lap and refused to meet his eyes. "A day and a half."

"I rest my case."

"But Greg had something come up at the office."

"That probably could've been easily handled by someone *at* the office. Not trying to be mean, but I still don't see what you see in him."

"Greg's nice."

"Yes, he is, but nice and boring shouldn't be what you settle for, sweetheart."

She looked away. In reality she had been a trifle disappointed by the abrupt end to what was supposed to have been a long relaxing weekend in Cancun, but they'd both taken work along, so they hadn't really planned to do that much relaxing. His having to head back let her return to work, as well.

"Have you two set a date yet?"

She shook her head tightly.

"Okay," he replied quietly. "I'm sorry. I'll turn off the interrogation lights. You called via Skype to share good news, not to be criticized by your old man."

She showed a small smile and tried not to dwell on her father's assessment of her life because she knew he meant well. "So, tell me what you've been up to."

They spent a few minutes talking about the movie shoot he was on in Peru, then he regaled her with all he'd seen and done. "The mountains are amazing! I'm planning to come back down here just as soon as I can find the time. You should come with me."

"I'd like that."

He didn't look as if he believed she'd actually come through, but he let it go. She was thankful.

"I need to get going, but let me ask you one thing."

"Ask away."

"What did you have at Hector's last night for dinner—the wrap and salad you always order?"

"Yes, I did, why?"

"You're in a rut, baby girl."

She sighed. "No, I'm not. I like the wrap and the salad."

"You've ordered that every time you and I've eaten there for the past what—two years? You know what I pray for?"

She chuckled. "No, what?"

"That some kind of way, you run into a situation that knocks your socks off and makes you see life from a whole new set of eyes."

"Bye, dad. I love you."

He grinned. "Love you, too. And try to enjoy Hawaii."

"Yeah, yeah," she said, matching his grin and signing off.

That night while lying in bed, Anita mentally replayed their conversation. In spite of his assessment, she didn't consider herself to be in a rut. She simply liked her life uneventful. Ordering the same dish from a menu didn't constitute a rut—or did it? Being with Greg didn't constitute settling—or did it? Admittedly, Greg wasn't the most gregarious or adventurous person in the world but then again, neither was she. Growing up with her mom in their Manhattan high-rise, she'd had a well-ordered, drama-free existence that consisted of school, music lessons and church on Sundays. She hadn't had a lot of friends, and those she did were on the same track of high achievement. They'd grown up to be doctors, lawyers, senators and other people of distinction. None had ever been busted for drugs, drinking or mooning. Her mother considered Greg an ideal catch because his PhD parents had raised him with the same goals. He might be boring but she'd never have to worry about him cheating on her, which was the reason for the divorce of her parents. Her father once said being married to Diane Whitehall was like living with an ice tray. Anita knew Greg loved her, but there was definitely none of the heat in the relationship that would make anyone mistake it for the stuff of one of Val's romance novels, and she was okay with that. They slept together but were in agreement that there was more to life than sex.

So she decided her dad was wrong. Her life didn't need shaking up. Randall Hunt was a creature of surprise and excitement but she had her mother's steady one-note genes and she was okay with that, as well. She checked her phone to see if Greg had responded to her earlier text. Nothing. She turned over and went to sleep.

Chapter 3

Pilot Steve Blair hated L.A.—the smog, the fast pace, the concrete, but he needed L.A. to stay in business, which was why he was setting down the small Gulfstream jet that evening at the Van Nuys municipal airport twenty miles outside the city. Ferrying big-money types from California to Hawaii's high-priced playgrounds on behalf of a Honolulu-based outfit was the straw that stirred his economic drink. Working for them ensured he could afford to run his chopper tour business at a loss and still live and enjoy life in the Aloha State on his own terms. He and the copilot, Cheri Davis, would be picking up a lone passenger in the morning, a woman named Hunt.

After taxiing to the area outside the single hangar, he and Cheri went through the checklist to shut down the plane. Cheri was a petite, coffee-colored woman originally from New Orleans. She'd earned her wings with the air force and, like Steve, hired herself out to supplement her income.

"I'm going to miss flying with you, Cheri."

Tomorrow would be her last run. She was getting married next month and moving back to her native Louisiana. "I'll miss you, too, Steve, but the rest of my life calls."

They'd been flying together for a few years, and he liked her because she was no-nonsense, knew her way around an aircraft and always showed up for the job alert and on time.

Cheri said, "I'll take care of the lockdown and meet you back here in the morning."

"You're not coming in to say bye to Ferg?"

"Uh, no. If you need to get in touch, just text me. I'll be at my sister's in L.A."

Ferguson Parker was also a Hawaii-based pilot but was temporarily manning the hangar's office. He and Cheri had had an ill-fated love affair a few years back. He had broken her heart and she'd had nothing to say to Ferg since. Steve always felt bad about how things had turned out because he'd introduced them. "I'll see you tomorrow then."

He grabbed his backpack and headed for the office.

Steve and Ferg were marine buddies who met during boot camp at Parris Island. They'd also served together during the hellhole that was Iraq. Like Steve, Ferg was in his late thirties, but unlike Steve, Ferg was blond and blue. Both men lived on the island of Kauai—Steve with his landlady, Mrs. Tanaka aka Mrs. T, and Ferg in the wide-open emptiness of Waimea Canyon.

When Steve entered the office, Ferg was seated at his desk, his attention on the screen of a laptop.

"Hey, Ferg."

"Hey, Cap. How was your flight in?"

"Easy."

"Cheri with you?"

"Yeah, but she's gone to her sister's place for the night."

Ferg shook his head. "I really screwed up with her, didn't I?"

"Yeah, you did. She's getting married next month, so tomorrow will be her last run with me."

"If I could do it over—" His voice trailed off.

Steve was of a mind that if Ferg was given a second chance, he'd do right by Cheri, but life rarely handed out seconds and besides, Cheri had moved on.

Ferg shut down the computer. "Let's get something to eat."

They chose a steak house not far from the hangar, and once they were seated and placed their orders, they caught up on their respective lives. "How's the dog?" Ferg asked while downing his beer.

Steve looked up from the baked potato he was filling with butter. "Fine. Left him with Mrs. T." The dog was a large male Rottweiler appropriately named Dog. Steve was technically his owner but they often shared custody.

"Good. How's your mom and dad?"

"They're good." Steve's family was in the oil business and had been since the early twentieth century. Ferg's folks owned a construction firm in Iowa. Coming from such different backgrounds it was hard to fathom why they were friends, but serving their country and having each other's back in the midst of the horror and carnage of Iraq made them close as brothers. At one time, there'd been three of them: Steve, Ferg and David Tanaka, but David lost his life to an IED in the streets of Baghdad and nothing was ever the same for the two friends he had left behind.

"So when are you coming home?" Steve asked.

"In a few days, hopefully—if the old man doesn't let that young girl kill him."

Steve laughed. The hangar's owner, a World War II vet named Tate was touring Europe with his thirty-year-old bride. Ferg had been running the place for the past two weeks, and this was Steve's first time seeing him since he had left the island. "Do you want me to do a flyby of your place next time I go up?"

"Yeah, that would be great. Make sure things are all right." He cut into his steak. "Damn I miss home."

Steve understood. The island of Kauai had a way of getting into your blood. Every time he was away from the island for more than a few days, a yearning to return would set in and all he could think about were the mountains, the ocean and the stars blanketing the night sky.

After their meal, Ferg gave Steve a ride, pulled up into the parking lot of the motel he'd been staying in while away from home. Steve had a reservation for the night there, also.

Ferg asked, "Do you want to ride in with me in the morning?"

"Yeah, I'd appreciate it. Save me cab fare."

"You are so cheap."

"My great granddaddy didn't make his fortune wasting money on cabs."

"You can't take that money or that oil with you, you know."

"Just turn off the car, farm boy, so we can go inside."

"I got your farm boy. You're going to be real mad in the morning when I leave your ass."

"Yeah, right. I can see you now trying to explain to Cheri why I'm a no-show."

Ferg's head dropped. When he raised it, his face held a grin that matched Steve's. "That was so cold. Does your mama know how cold and cheap you are?"

"Leave my mama out of this before I call yours and tell her Cheri kicked you to the curb because you couldn't keep your pants zipped up."

They both knew how much his mother had liked Cheri and how disappointed she'd been when the breakup had happened.

"Get out of my car."

The next morning, they grabbed a fast-food breakfast and

were in the office eating when Ferg's desk phone rang. As he
finished the conversation, he said to Steve, "That was Ernie.
He picked up your fare and is on his way back. Should be
here in a few minutes."

Ernie was Old Man Tate's brother-in-law and served as
the driver for people needing transportation to and from the
hangar.

"Aah, here he is now."

Steve turned to the window and saw a glistening black
town car pull up. Ernie, eighty years old if he was a day,
jumped out and hurried around to open the passenger-side
door. Out swung a pair of black stilettos attached to two
lean chocolate-brown legs so toned and taut they could only
be described as gams. The rest of her exited next, showing
Steve a slamming red business suit with a tastefully snug,
short skirt. The attire screamed power and it draped the nice
curvaceous body of a woman of average height. Her hair,
straight and cut short, framed a gorgeous brown face hidden
by high-end sunglasses.

Ferg asked, "How much you want to bet she's cold as
Juneau in January?"

Steve silently agreed. A woman exuding all that juice probably froze men in their tracks on a regular basis, but he didn't
do corporate ice maidens. He left the big-money babes to his
investment banker brother, Kyle.

Moving forward with a walk that mesmerized, she was
talking on her phone as she followed Ernie who was pulling
her suitcase to the door. She entered the office while saying,
"I know, Mother. I think this whole vacation idea's ridicu-
lous, too, but if you had told me when we talked the other day
that you were coming out here, I'd've delayed leaving until
tomorrow, but I'm on my way to the plane now."

She stopped speaking for a moment to say to Ferg standing
behind the counter, "Hello, I'm Anita Hunt. Is the pilot here?"

Ferg inclined his head Steve's way and his gaze locked with hers; her fancy shades to his mirrored aviators. She glanced away as if unimpressed and resumed her phone conversation. "Okay, Mother. I'll call you when I land. Bye."

She asked Steve, "Are we ready?"

"Whenever you are. Name's Steve Blair by the way."

"Nice to meet you," she said sounding exactly the opposite. "Where do I go?"

"Follow me. Later, Ferg."

Steve reached out to grab the handle of her bag only to be told frostily, "I got it, just show me to the plane."

He paused in response to the impatience in her voice and offered up a small shrug. "Understood."

Throwing Ferg a silent look, Steve strode out the door that led into the cavernous hanger. She trailed behind. Since she didn't seem to want his assistance, he didn't warn her that there might be oil on the hangar floor, and to be careful of her footing. And sure enough, he heard a surprised cry and turned back just in time to see her in the air and landing on her sweet, red-suited behind. She had such a startled look on her face, he forced himself not to smile as he explained quietly, "Sometimes the mechanics miss a few spots when they mop up the oil."

She set her hands to brace herself so she could rise only to place both palms in the small oil slicks she'd slipped on. "Dammit!" she hissed, looking down at the oil stains.

Holding on to his amusement yet again, he waited for her next move.

She eyed him critically. "After you've finished laughing, do you think you can find me some toweling to clean off my hands?"

"I'm not laughing." He watched her stand.

Now when someone falls their first instinct is to wipe off their behind and she did, but upon realizing she'd swiped her oily hands over the back of her snug red skirt, she snarled again, "Dammit!"

He decided she was the best entertainment he'd had in a while.

"This suit cost me a fortune," she cried.

"What do you do for a living?"

"I'm a lawyer, and the owner of this hangar should be sued for maintaining a hazardous enterprise."

"Typical lawyer response—a lawsuit."

A much lesser man might have withered under the ice that lasered from the fancy shades, but when you've been to war, an oil-streaked cutie whining because of a ruined suit didn't amount to much, if anything at all. And because playing butler wasn't part of his job, he told her. "Ladies' room's over there. You can wash your hands inside. I'll wait until you get back."

Anita stormed off. She was so upset she wanted to stamp her feet. If Blair's not-so-hidden smile were any indication, she'd given him quite a show. How humiliating. Not to mention she was going to have to change clothes. You don't arrive at a five-star resort looking like you've been working on engines all morning. This was her mother's fault for calling at the crack of dawn to demand Anita pick her up at the L.A. airport later today so she could attend a judicial conference. The reason she'd not mentioned it earlier was because Diane wanted her visit to be a surprise. Some surprise.

The inside of the restroom was just large enough to turn around, and mercifully clean. Anita spent a few minutes washing her hands before wriggling out of the skirt. The sight of the big blotch of oil spread over the seat left her so dismayed she chucked it into the trash receptacle because her dry cleaner would never be able to remove such an ugly stain.

Managing to open her large suitcase within the too-small confines took some skill but a few minutes later, she was dressed in a pair of gray silk pants and a sleeveless white silk blouse. There were fold lines in the garments from their stay in the suitcase but she hoped they'd be less noticeable by the time she touched down in Hawaii. Remembering the pilot was out in the hangar waiting, she chucked her oil-covered heels, too, pushed her painted toes into a pair of designer sandals then zipped the suitcase. Giving her makeup a quick glance in the tiny mirror over the sink, she hurried out to join him, and this time watched where she stepped as she pulled the wheeled suitcase in her wake.

He was standing with his arms folded, but because of the aviators she couldn't tell whether the pose was one of impatience, or if he stood that way habitually. Even though she preferred her men clean shaven and in suits, he exuded a sensual confidence that was all male. He was wearing a nice white shirt and pressed brown khakis. He was lean and fit, and sported just a shadow of a beard on his cheeks. He was so good-looking, he could have been on the cover of one of the romance novels Val George was always reading at lunch.

"You ready?"

She swore he was still laughing and she didn't like starring in embarrassing situations. "Yes."

"Follow me."

Onboard, Anita met the copilot, Cheri Davis. Blair then led her back into the well-appointed tan-and-cream-toned passenger cabin.

There were ten empty seats and she wondered if there would be more fliers. "How many other passengers will there be?"

"You're it, so sit wherever you like."

She chose a window seat midway down the aisle.

"It'll be about a six-hour flight," he said next. "Movies are there. Headphones, too."

Determined to ignore the unsettling heat that seemed to be emanating from him, she glanced at the monitor and other paraphernalia tucked in the seat back facing hers. He appeared to be silently studying her from behind his aviators and she wished he'd go to the cockpit, so she could pull herself together.

"Restrooms are in the back. If you get hungry, there are sandwiches and drinks in the galley, but wait until I say it's okay to move around before you check it out."

She nodded.

"You didn't hurt yourself when you fell, did you?"

His serious tone caught her off guard. She shook her head tightly. "No."

"Good. I'd've warned you about the oil but you didn't act like you wanted my input."

"And I certainly paid for that, didn't I? Hope you enjoyed it."

"You always so frosty, Counselor?"

Her chin rose. "Don't you have some place to be, Mr. Blair?"

He had the nerve to smile. "Yes, ma'am, I do. Any questions before we get under way?"

"No."

"Enjoy your flight." He met her eyes for a beat longer and made his exit.

She sighed and hoped that would be their last encounter. Something about him rubbed her the wrong way. It was bad enough that she was on her way to a place she'd rather not be. The last thing she needed was an irritating pilot with an overwhelming presence.

Chapter 4

Six hours later the plane banked over the island of Kauai and made its descent. From her window Anita took in the view of the populated area below and initially was not impressed, but the sight of the ocean and the mountains looming in the distance took her breath away. She'd seen the Pacific Ocean off the coast of California many times, and it always looked so primal and angry with the waves breaking against the Malibu coast, and of course she'd seen nothing but ocean for the duration of the flight, but this stretch was so placid and so blue it looked as if it were basking in the sparkling Hawaiian sunshine.

Blair's voice came over the speakers. "Welcome to Kauai, Ms. Hunt. Please fasten your seat belt. We'll be landing shortly."

The sight of the beaches, the lush tropical green and the knowledge that she'd have an opportunity to explore this paradise for ten days momentarily banished her pique at being forced to leave L.A. Admittedly, she wanted to whip out her phone and check in with the office to make certain things were going as they should, but as the descent continued that desire grew less and less. There was a small jolt as the wheels touched down onto the black asphalt runway and Anita Hunt, who'd never taken a true vacation, was in Hawaii.

Once the plane came to a halt, the female copilot entered the cabin. "How was the flight?"

"Fine, thanks."

"Is someone meeting you at the airport?"

"Yes, a rep from the resort where I'll be staying."

"Okay. If you'll follow me, I'll take you inside."

On the way out, she saw Blair seated in the cockpit at the plane's controls. He turned her way. "Enjoy Kauai, Counselor."

"Thank you."

Glad to put him and her embarrassment behind her, she followed Cheri down the steps and into the terminal.

The resort's representative was a brown-skinned older woman dressed in what Anita assumed to be traditional Hawaiian garb. As she placed a lovely flower lei around Anita's neck, she smiled and said, "Welcome to Hawaii, Ms. Hunt."

"Thank you."

"My name is Judith and I'll be driving the van that will take you to your resort. Your bags will be brought to your room."

Anita gave Cheri a thank-you and followed Judith to the van.

She boarded the air-conditioned van with a gaggle of people—couples, singles like herself and a few families with jet-lagged rambunctious children. That slightly alarmed her. She'd no idea she'd be going to a resort that catered to youngsters and that reawakened her pique. She slid into a seat behind a couple who appeared to be about her age. The guy was short and thin and wearing a loud print shirt. The woman with him was dressed in a nice sundress and flip-flops. She had her arm locked in his and was smiling up at him like he was her favorite dessert.

The woman turned around and unprompted said to her, "We're on our honeymoon."

Anita replied politely, "Congratulations."

"Thanks. This your first time in Hawaii?"

"Yes, it is."

"Us, too." She looked at her husband and said with a laugh, "Not that we'll be seeing anything outside of the room."

The husband elbowed his bride and they both giggled.

Anita blinked at the TMI—too much information—but noticed some of the other passengers react with indulgent smiles.

Hoping she wouldn't run into them with any kind of regularity, Anita pulled out her phone, then remembering Jane's edict not to call, she sighed and checked for a message from Greg. Nothing. He'd promised to get in touch when he had reached Tokyo. A part of her was starting to worry, but she told herself he'd probably gotten so wrapped up in work, he hadn't had the opportunity to send her a reply.

They were soon underway and Judith the driver steered them through a small residential area that could have been any small city in America. They passed a couple fast-food chains, a familiar retailer and much more traffic than she'd expected.

With the aid of a microphone, Judith began telling them about the resort. "It's situated on fifty acres on Poipu Bay."

She went on to talk about the amenities: the spa, the golf course, the myriad restaurants, oceanfront gazebos where you could sit and relax, and that there was even an on-site club that featured live jazz every evening. There were also exclusive adult-only areas and others designated solely for families and kids. As two children began squabbling with each other and filling the van with their arguing, Anita offered up a silent hallelujah that they'd be vacationing in the family area.

Judith continued with descriptions of the tide pools and waterfalls also on the property. "If this is your first visit to our paradise, I promise you it won't be your last."

Anita, thinking about what Jane and the others might be doing back at the office in L.A., thought Judith's claim debatable.

By then the subdivisions and stores had given way to open land and the tropical vistas she'd seen from the air. Once again, she was in awe. Stately palm trees and beautiful flowers of pinks and violets and oranges and reds competed for her visual attention. She took in the distant mountains and the pristine beaches they passed. The surroundings were so lush it was as if she'd been plunked down in the middle of a tropical rainforest.

The approach to the resort was through an avenue of towering palm trees interspersed with a variety of broad-leaved flowers with red and pink blooms. Judith stopped the van at the entrance and doormen in red coats and white pants were there to greet the new arrivals. Aided by a doorman's hand, Anita stepped down onto terra firma and the first thing she noticed was the fragrance in the air. She loved perfume and spent a great deal of money purchasing only the best, but nothing bottled came close to the exquisite floral scent of Hawaii.

"Welcome," the doorman said to her.

"Thank you."

"The concierge desk is inside and to your right."

She nodded and glanced around at the surrounding paradise as she followed the others from the van inside.

The lobby was beautiful. Stately columns of white marble showcased more palms and an expansive open-air space. It took only a few moments to check in and, once she'd signed all the necessary paperwork and received her room key, a bellman led her out into the fragrant air again for the short walk to her home for the next ten days.

It was more like a small single-family home than a hotel suite. He stuck the key in the door and gestured her in. The first thing she saw was the jewel-blue ocean and the sight drew her across the living room and out onto the grillworked veranda to get an up close look. How any place could be more beautiful with every passing moment was beyond her. No matter where she looked, her eyes took in something outstanding. She'd never experienced anything quite like this before.

"Your bags will be here momentarily," the bellman told her. "Let me give you a quick tour of the space and then you can relax."

Up a short flight of stairs was a large elegantly dressed bedroom and a connecting bath with multiple jets built into the shower wall. The bedroom had its own veranda and, like the one downstairs, there was a table and chairs to sit at and enjoy the view. She could see other guest spaces to the left and right but none were close enough to impede on anyone's privacy or glorious view.

Back downstairs to the living room with its flat screen and comfortable sofa and armchairs, and a dining area complete with table and chairs and a small powder room. Anita had been fortunate enough to stay in hotels all over the world, but nothing equaled this.

The bellman spent a few more minutes acquainting her with a map of the grounds. Once he had her oriented to her approval, she tipped him and he left her alone in her ocean-front abode.

She had no idea how long she stood on the veranda mesmerized by the water but she shook herself free and called her father and then her mother to let them know she'd arrived safely. After that she shot Greg a text relating the same info. Done, she unpacked and took out Jane's to-do list. On it were a number of things but at the top was massage. That was something Anita had never experienced before so she called the concierge to get information on what she needed to do.

Although she found the place beautiful and all, she was still in Hawaii under protest and the sooner she checked off the items on the list—like take a helicopter tour of the island and watch a sunset at some place called Polihale Beach—the sooner she'd be done with it, and maybe able to go home a few days early.

Steve parked his Jeep in the driveway of Mrs. Tanaka's rambling old house and got out. She lived in the middle of nowhere on the western side of the island off Route 50. She was a retired school teacher and the last living descendant of an old Japanese family that had come to the islands in the late 1800s to work the sugar cane plantations. The house was next to impossible to find unless you knew where to look because it was all but covered by the tropical landscape and the Japanese honeysuckle vines surrounding it. Needless to say, she had no neighbors and her preference for solitude was something she and Steve shared.

On the porch, he bowed reverently to the statue of the crossed-legged Buddha sitting so serenely atop its stone pedestal before knocking on the screened door. "Mrs. T. You home?"

She appeared at the door and as always welcomed him with a smile. "Well, hello." She held open the door. He paused to place a kiss on her unlined cheek before moving past her and into the front room. Unlike the riotous tropical jungle outside, the home's interior was as spartan as a warrior's. Simple functional furniture, a lone lamp and a short-legged table were the extent of the contents.

It felt good to be home again. Although he was as close as

a son could be to his parents in Texas, he loved Mrs. T, too. "How'd he do while I was gone?"

"Just fine. He's out on the porch."

The "he" was Dog, the sixty-five-pound male Rottweiler. Dog had originally belonged to Mrs. Tanaka's son, David, but his death in Iraq left the Rott—who'd been adopted as a starving pup off the streets of Baghdad—without a master and Steve and Ferg without one of their best buddies. They'd made David a promise that, if anything happened to him, they'd take Dog to his mother in Hawaii. So they had honored the vow by bringing Dog with them to David's funeral. The canine and the mother took an instant liking to each other which she attributed to David's scent being in the house, but she also took an instant liking to Steve and he to her. In the end, she took Dog in, and when Steve and Ferg declined the offer from the marines to reenlist because they'd had enough war, she took Steve in, as well. He lived in the old cottage on the back of her property. Both he and Ferg fell in love with the quiet beauty of Kauai. Each could have chosen to return home but opted not to. It was as if they'd needed the island to heal.

When Dog saw Steve step onto the porch, he bounded over and immediately lifted himself up for a head rub which Steve affectionately gave. "How are you, buddy? You take good care of Mrs. T while I was gone?"

The two roughhoused a bit before Steve took a seat on the edge of the porch and Dog stretched out on his belly beside him. Draping an arm across Dog's thick neck, Steve gazed over the mountains towering against the horizon. He swore if you listened hard enough you could hear the hidden waterfalls even though they were miles away. "I never get tired of this view."

"Neither do I. Let me get you some juice and you can tell me about the run."

Over a chilled glass of papaya juice, Steve told her about

the routine flight to L.A. "A quick trip there and back with an overnight thrown in. Nothing special—except the lawyer in the stilettos."

Mrs. T was rocking in an old cane chair. "Stilettos? Was she pretty?"

He shrugged and smiled inwardly. She was always trying to find him a lady friend. When he had first moved in, she'd invited over every eligible young woman within fifty miles for dinner. "I guess. A bit too icy for my tastes though."

"So what happened with her?"

He told her about being rebuffed in his attempt to help the lawyer with her bag, and about her slipping and falling in the oil.

"You didn't laugh, did you, Steve?"

"Not out loud, no."

"Was she hurt?"

"Just her ego."

"Why would anyone wear stilettos to Kauai?"

Another shrug. "Maybe she's here for a big meeting. I don't know."

Apparently Mrs. T didn't see the lawyer as a prospect because she changed the subject. "You flying in the morning?"

"Yep. Doing runs for the resort. Won't know how many though until I get there." He'd been piloting helicopter tours for four years. He loved flying, always had, but the war had dampened his feelings for a while. Now that he didn't have to dodge weapons fire anymore, it was again his one true love. He stretched his arms and shoulders in response to the weariness he felt. "I'm going to get going. I need a nap and I promised my mother I'd call her today."

"Give Lady Gwendolyn my love."

The two women had become close over the years. "Will do. See you later?"

"Only if you want the spaghetti and meatballs I'm cooking for dinner."

"I'll see you later."

He stepped off the porch, and with Dog trotting by his side, made his way down the vine-choked path to his home.

Mrs. Tanaka's land was once part of a sugar cane plantation, and the house Steve lived in had been built for the caretaker. It had one bedroom, one bathroom and a small kitchen. David had used it as his bachelor pad during the summers he was home from college and, when Steve had claimed the space for himself, it was in good shape. The flowering vines and tropical vegetation were as prevalent around his place as they were around Mrs. Tanaka's but Steve and his chain saw made sure they didn't get out of hand.

Inside the house, he dumped his backpack on the worn sofa and called his mother. Cell service was spotty so he used the landline and put it on speaker. "Hey, Mom."

"Hey. How's my favorite fly guy?"

He grinned and patted Dog on the head and took a seat at the kitchen table near the phone. "Doing good. How're you?"

"Can't complain."

They spent a few minutes chitchatting about his younger brother, Kyle, and the investment firm he owned, and about Steve's dad, Marcus, and her never-ending battle to get him to retire. "He'll retire when he's ready, Mom. Why do you keep hassling him?"

"Because I want him to retire with me, not to a casket."

His dad was in his late sixties and still going strong as CEO of Blair Oil, the company founded by Steve's great-grandfather. "He'll be fine. Oh, Mrs. T says hello."

"Tell her hello from this end. You coming home for Juneteenth?"

"I'm planning to."

"Okay. And by the way, I saw Yvette Jenison at the market yesterday. I still want to strangle her."

"Let it go."

"I have, and I was polite because your grandmother raised me right, but I wanted to shove her into the milk cooler—selfish little witch. You don't send my son a Dear John letter while he's serving his country in Iraq."

The pain of that day rose inside, but he let it wash over like a wave over a surfer. "How's she doing?"

"I didn't ask."

He chuckled. "So what else is going on?"

They spent a few more minutes talking about how much she was enjoying the new reverend at their A.M.E. church, then about the fall his Aunt Charlene took a few days ago while riding one of her horses and how blessed she was not to have broken any bones. After a few more topics that left him amused at her talkativeness, she said, "I don't want to keep you. I'll call you in a few days."

"That'll be great. Tell Dad, hey. Love you, Mom."

"Love you more."

As he sat in the silence, Yvette Jenison's beautiful face floated across his mind's eye. They'd hooked up during their first year at UT, but he hadn't been happy there. Too restless a spirit he supposed, so rather than waste any more of his parents' money, he had left school at the beginning of his sophomore year, and signed the paperwork to become a marine. Yvette had been both angry and hurt, but in the end gave the impression that she supported his decision and would continue to love him while he was away. Six weeks after he had arrived in Baghdad, her letter arrived saying she'd met someone else and hoped he understood.

Of course, he wasn't the first soldier to be ditched, but having a lady back home was sometimes the only sane thing to hold on to in the insanity of war. It hurt. Hurt bad. In many ways it still did, which was one of the reasons he hadn't opened his heart to anyone else. That and the fact that he'd yet to meet a woman who wanted to live in an overgrown cottage in the middle of a rainforest with a Rottweiler and a little Japanese-American lady with a fondness for spaghetti and meatballs.

Chapter 5

Anita had to admit that waking up to the sight and sounds of the ocean was an incredible way to begin the day. The breeze gently lifted the thin white curtains and filled the room with the scent of ocean water and the signature fragrance of the rich Kauai air. Getting up, she also admitted to feeling more relaxed than she ever remembered and she chalked it up to yesterday evening's incredible massage and the soak afterward in the spa's heated lava-rock pool. The spa was a resort all to itself, with both private and semiprivate massage areas, an enormous pool and, like everything else on the grounds, it was surrounded by tropical beauty.

Getting up, she walked barefoot onto the veranda. The breeze felt good on her skin. Fat clouds tinted with predawn pinks and mauves hung over the horizon. Today's agenda would begin with breakfast followed by a helicopter tour. Like the spa and massage, the tour was one of the items on Jane's to-do list. Anita had never flown in a helicopter but she enjoyed flying, so in a way she was looking forward to it, if only to be able to cross it off the list.

After a shower and a delightful breakfast of quiche and fruit, courtesy of room service, she checked her phone and found a text message from Greg. Smiling, she opened it and read:

> Anita. I know this is taking the coward's way out but I didn't have the courage to tell you face-to-face. I'm breaking off our engagement so that I can marry Marie Bates, my office mate. She's everything I want in a wife. She's smart, spontaneous and a lot of fun. I know I'm going to catch hell from my parents and probably you too for this decision, but she's the woman I want in my life. I know I've hurt you terribly and I hope that one day you can forgive me. Sincerely, Greg.

Wide-eyed, legs weak, she read it again. This had to be a joke, but Greg had no sense of humor whatsoever, so she dropped down into the nearest chair and tried to catch her breath. She was stunned, speechless. For a moment, her entire being seemed to go blank. She read the message again.

A thousand questions filled her mind. How long had he been seeing Marie? How long had he loved her? But in the end it didn't matter. She'd been dumped by a man she thought she knew; a man she'd called herself in love with since being escorted by him to her deb ball during high school. And now, she'd been kicked to the curb for the smart, spontaneous and lots-of-fun Marie.

Parts of her wanted to strangle him for putting her through this and yes, his mother was going to give him hell. Anita hoped Marie had a tough hide because Sylvia Ford was going to go after her with an elephant gun, and Anita's mother, Diane, would be handing her the bullets. Anita allowed her-

self a small smile at the absurdity of the situation. Her mother
was going to have a stroke! Her father was going to laugh
himself silly.

Personally, Anita was still too stunned to put a name to
her own feelings, but honestly, deep inside, there was a sense
of relief. Yes she was hurt, humiliated and the rest, but now
for maybe the first time in her life, there'd be no Greg pressuring her to find a job on the East Coast or questioning her
decisions about what was right for her future. That he'd probably rushed back to the hotel the night they had dinner, not
for work but for the woman waiting there, made her furious,
but Marie could have him.

Anita had herself and a damn good job. Reality said that
she'd grieve the end of this decades-long relationship and she
probably would, but for now, she was moving on. Her goal
was to get this damn vacation out of the way so she could fly
home and do her best to change Jane's words from *considering* to *recommending.* And as for Greg—he could kiss her ass!

She took the time to send her parents word of the broken
engagement. Once that was done, she picked up her small
cross-shoulder bag and walked through the early sunshine
to meet the van taking her to the helicopter tour.

The trip to the airfield was a short one but it seemed like
an eternity because the two squabbling children from yesterday and their parents were also in the van. They appeared
to be seven or eight—Anita had no real way of gauging their
true ages—but it was certain their parents had no control. The
boy and girl were going at each other like wet cats in a bag
and, no matter how many times the parents implored them
to behave, they were ignored.

When the van pulled up to the hangar, she couldn't wait
to get out. She knew from talking with the concierge that
the choppers' sizes varied. Some didn't have a lot of seating
space so she prayed the family would be on a separate flight.

She got her wish, but sometimes it pays to be careful what you ask for. The agent informed her that she would be flying alone and that her pilot would meet her in a few minutes. She thanked the heavens, but her relief was cut short when Steve Blair, wearing the aviators, came striding toward her with a clipboard in his hand.

"So, Counselor, we meet again."

She raised a perfectly arched brow above her sunglasses. "You're my pilot?"

"Yes, ma'am."

She sighed audibly and noted he had the nerve to grin— again. He also had the nerve to be even better looking than he'd been on the flight out of L.A., if that was possible. The business khakis had been replaced by green army camo pants with pockets on the legs. His brown, long-sleeved shirt was unbuttoned allowing her to see a white tank with USMC printed on the front. A silver chain around his neck accented the hollow of his bared throat. Realizing she was staring at the space, she quickly raised her gaze.

"Are you ready?" he asked.

She swore he was laughing—again. He had a soft voice tinted with a Southern flavor that seemed to reach inside and stroke her soul. Startled by the thought, she shook it off. "Yes."

"This way."

As they walked to where the bird sat waiting, Steve didn't know why seeing her again made him feel so good, but it did. Although she hadn't said more than a dozen words to him since their initial meeting, he found himself wanting to know what made the prickly lady lawyer tick. From her continued frosty attitude, he doubted such info would be forthcoming, which was one of the reasons he didn't do high-powered, all-work, no-play women, no matter how gorgeous they were, and she certainly was all that and a bag of chips, but she interested him just the same.

"Are you in Kauai for business or pleasure?"

"Neither."

That confused him and the look on his face must have relayed that.

"I'm here because my boss thought I needed a vacation."

"But you begged to differ, I'll bet."

"Give the man a cigar. How long does the tour last?"

"Depends on what you want to see and sometimes on the weather. If rain moves in, we'll have to head back."

"All right."

"So what do you want to see?"

"Doesn't matter."

He stopped and folded his arms over his chest. "You really don't want to be here, do you?"

"No. I have work back in L.A. that needs attention and, even though I'm the one who's supposed to be handling it, I was told not to call."

"Which means your boss has your back."

"Yes, but I don't like being kept out of the loop."

He took in the irritation on her face and the tense set of her bare arms in the red sleeveless shirt. Were she his employee, he'd've sent her on vacation, too. She was wound up as tight as his grandfather's old pocket watch. All that stress was liable to kill a girl, but he didn't say that for fear she'd punch him. "Okay, we'll see how it goes then."

It only took a minute for her to climb into the seat beside him and strap on her safety belt. He handed her a set of headphones with a connected mic so she'd be able to hear him over the rotors describing what they were seeing and just in case she had a comment and wanted to talk, which he doubted in light of her attitude.

He went through the preflight safety check and when everything was ready, guided the bird into the air. "We'll hop over to Kilauea first and say hello to Madam Pele," he yelled over the drone of the rotors. "No trip to Hawaii is complete without it." She didn't reply but he was okay with that.

A short while later they were over the most active volcano in the world. Anita was so awed she didn't know what to look at first—the gaping maw below with its glowing cauldron center that resembled passage to the underworld, the billowing plumes of smoke, or the creeping fat rivers of slow-moving lava.

He swung them around while telling her, "That large vent down there on Pele's backbone is named Pu'u O'o. It's the most active of all. The goddess has been flowing nonstop since the late eighties."

He directed her gaze to another vent spewing lava. "That one's named for Martin Luther King. It broke through around his birthday in 2004."

Anita was so blown away she couldn't find words.

"One more sight," he told her smiling.

Next she knew they were descending so she could get a better view of the veins of hot lava sliding off Pele's cliffs and crashing into the ocean. "That's how the black sand beaches are formed."

Anita had never seen anything so terrifying and yet so beautiful. It was like watching the birth of an alien world.

"Don't want to get too close," he voiced. "The lava hitting the water produces hydrogen sulfide gas."

She turned to him startled.

"We're okay up here, Counselor. Promise. Ready for the rest of the tour?"

Excitement sang in her veins. She nodded and gave him her first smile.

"Let's head back to Kauai. You ain't seen nothing yet."

And he was right. He swung them over the grand Kilauea

lighthouse and then rendered her speechless once again as he flew over the Wailua Falls. What looked like hundreds of tons of water poured down the cliffs. "They used those falls in the opening shots of that old-school show *Fantasy Island*."

That surprised her.

"Lots of movies were shot here. *Raiders of the Lost Ark. King Kong. Throw Momma from the Train*."

That earned him another smile. They buzzed another waterfall even more spectacular than the last. "Manawaiopuna Falls. Recognize it from *Jurassic Park?*"

Her wide eyes met his and his soft laugh came through her ears. "Yep, that's it. Impressed yet, Counselor?"

"Very much."

"Good, now for the big finale, my favorite spot on earth, Waimea Canyon."

Anita couldn't believe there was more. She'd also lost track of time. According to her watch, they'd been flying for more than an hour.

He flew west and all Anita could do was stare down as he presented her with the island's beauty. He'd said at one point that Kauai was known as the Garden Island and it was easy to see why. Waimea Canyon with its rugged peaks, high plateaus, deep green valleys and waterfalls was absolutely stunning.

"It's called the Grand Canyon of the Pacific. Fourteen miles long, one mile wide and more than 3,600 feet deep. We can't even see the parts that are under the ocean."

It looked like the old Hawaiian gods had scooped out the center of the land for miles around. Jagged hills that appeared to be made of centuries-old hardened lava sprang toward the sky beside other peaks made of red and brown earth. The canyon was enormous. She saw wind-eroded walls of striated stone and lava that resembled gigantic stands of carved Christmas trees. She stared down surprised at what appeared to be animals bounding up the side of a cavern. "Are those sheep?"

"Yes, ma'am. Most of the area is so wild, people can't get in, so there're quite a few up in these mountains if you know where to look. I'm going to swing over my buddy's place to make sure things are okay and then head us back to the coast."

A short few minutes later, he said, "Cabin's there. Can you see it? Belongs to the guy in the hangar office back in L.A."

She could but it looked like a flat-roofed doll's house against the vast open area surrounding it. He swung the chopper around and headed east. She was about to ask why anyone would live so far away from civilization when rain-drops began hitting the windshield and a gust came up that rocked the helicopter. She saw him peering at the sky and she did the same.

"Going to call the airport," he told her. He hit a button on the dash and said into the mic, "Hey, Max, what's going on weather-wise here at the canyon?"

The rain was steady now and the wind had picked up con-siderably.

Max was the weather tech at the airport at Lihue. "There's a front forming. Looks like a big one. Seems to be mov-ing pretty fast so I don't think it'll last too long, but there'll probably be damage. We're sending out an island-wide alert right now."

The rain was coming down harder.

"We're going to try and make it back. Tell the tower to pick us up on the scope if they can, just in case."

"Will do. Good luck."

Anita asked, "Trouble?"

"Maybe."

As if to counter the *maybe,* a big gust of wind suddenly blew hard from the west. "Make that a yes!" he stated.

And as he said that, wind, pouring rain and streaks of lightning replaced what had been, up to that moment, a beautiful and calm blue-sky day. Now it was dark and foreboding. She held on and tried to keep her panic under wraps. "Weather always this unpredictable?"

"For the most part."

She knew the last thing he needed was to be distracted by a bunch of inane questions, so she kept quiet, waited and watched.

"We need to get out of this. Going to swing back up to my friend's place. He has a chopper pad. We'll land and wait there until this blows over."

Anita nodded tightly while the chopper rocked and rolled in response to the furious wind, witchlike fingers of lightning flashing through the downpour and the answering bass booms of the thunder. Yes, landing would please her a lot. Even if they wound up in the middle of nowhere, it was better than being in the air at the mercy of the growing storm.

But wanting to land and doing so were two different things. The bird was pitching crazily due to the angry wind. Rain pelted the windshield so forcefully she hoped Blair could see because she couldn't see a thing. A flash of lightning exploded so closely she stifled a scream and gripped t. e armrest in reaction. A quick look behind her showed the copter's tail ablaze. Fear grabbed her and she looked to him anxiously.

"Not good!"

The wind was tossing them around like it was offended by their presence. His next words scared her even more than the fire.

"We're going down, Counselor! Brace yourself!"

Terrified, she prayed and swore if she died, she'd come back and haunt Jane Sheridan for the rest of her natural-born life. Then the chopper leveled out, but they were roaring through trees and foliage at a high rate of speed. Branches broke through the windows and windshield. Blinding rain poured in. She heard herself screaming and felt his iron arm holding her back in her seat, and she was still screaming because the nightmare seemed to go on forever, and then they crashed into something so solidly, the impact threw her forward and her head exploded with pain before everything went black.

Chapter 6

Anita came back to life slowly. When she opened her eyes, all she saw were trees. Everywhere. *Where am I?* The pounding in her head made it difficult to make sense of anything. Branches, leaves and pieces of glass covered her lap. She turned to the left and saw a man in the seat beside her. His head was tipped forward, his eyes closed. A thin rivulet of blood coursed down the side of his face. For a moment, the fog of confusion refused to let her brain do anything other than puzzle over his presence, and then her memory kicked in. Alarmed, her eyes flashed his way.

"Oh, my God!" Fighting the grogginess and the pain, she tried to reach him. "Please don't be dead. Please!"

She couldn't move though, and it took another minute to glean the reason. Her seat belt. She forced her disembodied fingers to undo the buckle. "Please don't be dead. God, please don't let him be dead!"

She pressed her palm against his heart but felt nothing. She leaned over and placed her ear against his chest. The strong steady beat flooded her with so much relief tears sprang to her eyes. Dashing them away, she saw his eyes flutter open. The brown orbs locked on her and she froze. He assessed her for a long, silent moment as if trying to figure out who she was, then as if it was the most natural thing to do, he ran a bent knuckle over the tear sliding down her cheek. "Why're you crying, Counselor?"

"I thought you were dead."

"Wouldn't mind going to heaven with you."

His crooked smile opened up a spot in her heart she never knew existed. What was it about him that affected her so? Grabbing hold of herself she backed out of range. "Do you remember the crash?"

He closed his eyes momentarily as though trying to make his memory work, then said, "Yeah. Shit!" He cursed softly. He felt blindly for his belt, unsnapped it and slowly struggled to sit up straight. "Damn, my head hurts. How're you?"

"Alive."

"That's a good thing."

"How do we get back to the resort?"

Steve checked her out. He wondered if she knew she had a knot on her head the size of Texas. "Let me get my bearing a minute." He took mental stock of his body. Nothing seemed to scream *broken,* but he was pretty banged up. His head was throbbing. He was sure he had a concussion. "You certain you're okay?"

"My head's pounding, but I'm breathing."

He looked over and gave her a small smile.

"What?"

"Figured a high-priced lady like yourself would be in hysterics by now."

"Since you don't know a thing about *a high-priced lady like myself,* I'm going to ignore that and ask again. How do we get back to the resort?"

Even though he knew this wasn't the time, he enjoyed baiting her. In response to her pointed question, he shrugged. "No idea, but it may take some doing."

Her mouth dropped. "Why?"

"There's no cell service out here because of the mountains so, being able to call on a standard phone for help will be problematic. The radar guys at the airport know we're out here, but unless they saw us drop off the scope, they're not going to know we're in trouble until we don't show up. The good news is my buddy Ferg has a satellite phone at his place, so if we can get there, we'll be able to make a call."

He peered out of what was left of the window, looking first up and then down in an effort to ascertain their position. It wasn't a good one, but at least the rain had stopped. "I'm going to need you to sit real still, Counselor."

"And the reason being?"

"I believe we're caught in the trees."

Her eyes went wide as plates and she quickly peered around as if to ascertain the truthfulness of his words.

Moving as gingerly as the aches and pains allowed, Steve attempted to open the battered door beside him, but it didn't budge. He surveyed the area by the door. From what he could make of things, there was a huge splintered limb wedged against it that was probably a companion to the big leafy branches filling the shattered windshield, and the ones taking up the backseat. In Iraq, he'd found himself in more sticky situations than he cared to remember. He'd even piloted a few choppers brought down by rocket-propelled grenades, but he'd never been stuck in a tree. And at the moment, he'd no way of knowing if they were a few feet off the ground, or hanging in the canopy a hundred feet up. Not good.

"So, what do we do?" she asked.

"The jarhead in me wants to rock this sucker and see if we can't shake loose."

"No! What's plan B?"

"Not sure yet. Maybe we can try and climb out, but there's no way of knowing how far up we are. Can you see the sky or the ground from over there?"

He waited while she peered through the leaves and limbs. "No."

"Nothing on this side, either. Let's try this." Ignoring whatever was paining his lower right leg, he tried to stand and the chopper immediately began to rock. He stopped.

Anita's heart pounded in her throat. "I don't think that's a good idea. Please sit down." She'd never been in a situation like this, and holding it together was hard. Hysteria seemed much more appropriate, but she didn't want to give him the satisfaction.

"I need you to do something for me."

She raised an eyebrow. "What?"

"I want you to try and stand. Need to see how the weight is distributed."

She wanted to argue *that didn't make sense,* but being in a helicopter wedged in by a bunch of trees made even less sense.

"Easy now," he cautioned.

Bracing one hand on the seat, Anita stood slowly. The copter didn't move.

"Weight's all on this side, then."

She sat down just as cautiously. "And that tells you what?"

He looked her in the eye.

She felt fear wanting to scream its way free. "You are not going to rock this thing! I'm not playing with death twice."

"Then we stay here and starve."

She looked away and blew out an exasperated breath. Granted, starving to death would keep her from getting back to L.A. and wringing Jane's neck, but what if they were killed by this jarhead plan? Starving to death or dying in a plunging helicopter. Some choice. She surrendered. "Okay. The jarhead plan it is."

He nodded grimly. "Put your belt back on and make sure it's good and tight."

She complied and watched him do up his own belt.

"We may drop fast, or it may be slow. For sure we're going to be bounced around."

Steve prayed this would work and they didn't crash and burn. He glanced her way. Her hard-set features were a mixture of fear and resolve. No hysteria for her. He liked that. "You ready?"

She nodded tightly and gripped the armrests.

Steve prayed again and threw his weight against the door. The pain in his messed-up shoulder exploded like a shot of lightning, but he gritted his teeth and kept pounding away until the bird began to rock. He hit the door hard one more time and they were falling.

Anita's terror clawed at her throat. She expected the chopper to plummet like a rock but as they bumped and bounced and ricocheted off trunks and branches, and the metal cried and shuddered, it was more like being in a pinball machine. The rain had apparently doused the tail fire but she kept envisioning them bursting into flames. As the chopper tumbled, the sheer scariness of it all made it hard to breathe. One moment the bird would catch on a large branch and come to a rest, only to have the branch snap a few seconds later and send them falling again. All around were sounds of snapping limbs and protesting leaves. Her heart was pounding and thoughts of dying rushed through her blood like white water over rapids. The impacts with the branches rattled her spine and snapped her teeth together.

"Don't bite your tongue!" he yelled through the chaos.

The warning registered but she couldn't respond. She was too busy praying and hanging on. After what seemed like a lifetime, they came to rest again, nose down and this time the stop held.

They both sat still as each held their breath. In the echoing silence, they shared a look.

As if her words might jar them loose, she asked softly, "Do you think we're on the ground?"

The trunks and limbs filling the interior when they woke up had come along for the ride, so there was no way of making an immediate determination.

Steve hesitantly undid his belt and raised up in the seat as best he could. The bird stayed put. He knew not to be too relieved but allowed himself a glimmer of hope. "See if your door will open. Easy now."

Anita tried her door. Because of the trees in her window it protested, but it opened. She wanted to sob with relief.

"Can you see anything?"

"Yes! There are still trees below us but I can make out the ground now." It was such a wonderful sight she wanted to cheer.

"Okay, good. That's better."

Steve thought for a moment as how to best end this mini adventure. He tried his door again. Still nothing. Hoping the chopper would stay put for a few more minutes, he began pushing the limbs and branches out of his busted window. He needed to be able to see for himself just how close to the ground they were. He noted that without being asked or told she began clearing her window, too. "Careful not to cut yourself on the glass."

She nodded and undid her belt. Removing her shoulder bag, she knelt on the seat with her back to him to give herself more leverage. He knew it was inappropriate, but ran admiring eyes over her lower anatomy in the snug white capris. He smiled to himself and returned his attention to what he was supposed to be doing.

It took a while but they finally managed to free the windows and what remained of the windshield of most of the excess foliage. Steve tried his door again. Like hers, it protested but it opened.

He could see the ground about forty feet below. The blood rushing to his aching head made him dizzy. He righted himself and sat back against the seat until the wooziness passed.

"Are you okay?" she asked in a concerned voice.

"Probably have a concussion but I can't worry about that now." He swung his head her way. "I've been in worse shape. I'll get you home in one piece. Promise." He then added, "Sorry about all this."

"Blair, you may be an arrogant man, but not even you can control the weather."

He nodded at the truth in her reply, then sat up. "Okay, Counselor, let's get the hell out of here." He thought about all the people who'd be worried by their absence: the resort people, her family, his family. He needed to get them to Ferg's cabin and as quickly as possible. Even if no one could rescue them right away, at least people would know they were safe.

"So how do we get to the ground?" she asked.

"We jump."

She stared again. "Jump?"

"I'll go first. Once I'm down, you jump and I'll catch you."

"Uhm."

"Don't worry. I'm a marine. Done this a thousand times. It'll be a piece of cake."

Anita thought this jarhead plan was as crazy as the last one.

"Trust me, okay?"

She didn't, but again what choice did she have.

"I'm pretty sure the bird's stable enough for me to leave you, so no sense in waiting around."

To her added horror, he raised himself in the seat. Before

she could blink, he was crouched on the edge of the door. "See you in a minute, Counselor."

And he jumped!

She scooted to the window and saw him hit the ground and roll. He got up dusted himself off and called up. "Come on down!" he yelled in a voice reminiscent of *The Price Is Right*.

She couldn't believe he had jokes! It made her smile but only for a moment. The thought of actually jumping scared her witless. He said he'd catch her but she didn't see that happening. What she saw instead was breaking both legs.

As if sensing her indecision, he called up again, "You've been a trouper so far, Anita. Don't punk out on yourself now! Try and relax when you jump."

Relax! Knowing if she didn't jump soon, the fear would totally paralyze her and she'd be stuck in the chopper until Christmas. So again, she prayed. Hard. And tried not to think about broken bones. Closing her eyes on one last prayer, Anita jumped.

As the ground rushed up to meet her, she held on to her scream. He caught her just as he'd promised. His strong arms latched on to her and the impact sent them both tumbling. When the world righted itself again, her happy eyes met his.

"Nice," he said.

Only then did she realize that she was stretched out on top of him, their bodies flush like lovers in bed. Instantly horrified, she jumped up and willed her thumping heart to stop.

He on the other hand propped himself on one elbow and looked up at her grinning. "Welcome to terra firma, Counselor."

She wanted to kick him, but instead, grated out, "Thank you."

"My pleasure."

Although her body still felt the hard heat of him, the last

thing her brain wanted to reference was anything having to do with pleasure—especially with him. "Where to now?"

He stood and she noticed that he was favoring one leg. "Are you hurt?" she asked.

"Yes, but I'll check it out once we get to the cabin."

Suddenly, the silence exploded with the sound of crunching metal and he grabbed her hand. "Run!"

Anita didn't have time to ask why, because he was already pulling her behind him like a kid with a kite. They were in a small clearing and were still running when a crash shook the surroundings. She looked back just in time to see the banged-up chopper plunge to the ground and burst into flames. The fireball was so bright she had to shield her eyes.

Steve sighed. That bird had served him well. He watched it burn. "Damn."

"My purse and phone are in there!" she cried.

"Too late. Sorry."

"You don't understand. My life is in that phone. All my contacts, the email addresses of my clients!" Greg's stupid email. "What am I supposed to do?"

"Start life over?"

"This is not funny!"

"Didn't say it was."

Anita wanted to curse whomever was responsible for this awful day. "So, now what?"

He looked around. "Not one-hundred-percent sure where we are, but I think we're close to the cabin."

"You think?" she asked doubtfully.

"Hey, it's better than saying, we're totally lost." He paused and studied her. She looked a mess. "Where's your sense of adventure?"

"I lost it when we crashed," she replied sullenly.

He shook his head. "You've got to learn to roll with the

punches, Counselor. Enjoy life a little more. We're alive. That's what counts."

Anita was grateful to be alive but, at the moment, she didn't give a damn about adventure. All she wanted was off this merry-go-round so she could return to the resort, have another massage, a hot shower and a chilled glass of expensive wine, and then fly home, but instead, this vacation from hell would now involve an extended trek through the wilderness. "Which way?"

Steve thought she was a hard nut to crack. He looked up at the sky. It was still gray and cloudy, so using the sun to steer by was out, thus he relied on his inner compass and hoped it was accurate. "West."

And when she marched off in the proper direction, he chuckled to himself.

Chapter 7

Anita didn't know east from west, and had no idea if she was going the right way, but because he didn't stop her, she kept marching through the foggy tree-lined valley. Behind the trees, mist-shrouded cliffs rose heavenward in staggered, ragged columns, making the place seem cut off from the world beyond.

It occurred to her that he might not be saying anything just to watch her walk around in circles, but she put that out of her mind and plowed ahead. Granted, the surroundings were incredibly beautiful and the silence serene, but she'd had her fill of beauty and serenity. After the harrowing day, all she wanted was L.A.'s smog, crowds and bumper-to-bumper traffic.

Plus, the grass she was walking through was wet and, because she was wearing sandals, so were her feet. Had she been informed back at the resort that by midafternoon she'd almost be killed in a helicopter crash, she'd've opted for sturdier footwear, but seeing as how no warning had been given, she might as well be barefoot for all the protection the sandals provided.

She wanted to curse, scream and jump up and down like a two-year-old throwing a tantrum, but that wouldn't change anything, so she kept moving and hoped the sun would come out to beat back the chilly damp air and maybe dry her wet clothes.

She thought back on the conversation she'd had with her father and his wish for her to be in a situation that rocked her world. She hoped he was happy because she was so out of her element, she might as well be walking on the moon. Glancing back over her shoulder, she saw that Blair had picked up a large branch and was using it as a cane to aid his injured leg. The sight deflated the sense of bitchy selfishness she'd wrapped herself in since this whole hellified situation began. In truth, she was so grateful not to be out here alone. Without him, she wouldn't've survived and she owed him her thanks instead of the bad attitude she'd been subjecting him to. Greg's email was adding its share, but Blair had nothing to do with that, either. She stopped and waited for him to catch up.

"What's the matter?" he asked.

"Me."

Confusion creased his brow.

"I've been acting like a three-year-old when I should be telling you how grateful I am for all you've done for me today. Thank you," she added quietly.

Admittedly, Steve's first thought was that she was delirious from the bump on her head, but the sincerity in her eyes and how utterly miserable she appeared made him take her seriously. "I appreciate that, but don't worry about it. Like I said earlier, you've been awesome. No whining, no tears, no hysterics. Couldn't ask for a better partner in this mess."

He thought he saw tears in her eyes just before she turned

away. When she faced him again she said softly, "You're very kind. I'd like for us to start over, if we can."

He wasn't sure what she meant.

She stuck out her hand. "Hi. I'm Anita Hunt. Pleased to meet you."

His lips curved into a smile, and he shook her hand. "Steve Blair. Nice meeting you, as well."

"Where're you from?"

"Texas. You?"

"Born in New York, but, after my parents split, I spent my summers in L.A. with my father."

"Siblings?"

"None. You?"

"One. Younger brother named Kyle." He searched her face and decided he liked this version of her. "Feel better?"

She nodded. "I do. Thank you."

Something grew between them at that moment. They seemed to be seeing each other in a new light. He wasn't sure what it meant, but sensed she felt it, too, because she looked him over hesitantly before asking, "What's going on with your leg?"

"Wrenched my knee in the crash. Jumping out of the bird didn't help."

"Then how about we walk slower."

"Good idea."

"Anything I can do to help?"

"Not unless you can carry me."

"I'm appreciative, but not that much."

He liked it when she smiled.

"How much farther?" she asked.

"Probably another hour's worth of walking."

She sighed in response but followed it with, "Then let's keep this adventure rolling."

Yeah, he liked this version much better.

As they walked, they talked about everything and nothing: her firm and the impending partnership; how long he'd had the tour business, and why he'd never live on the mainland again.

He told her, "This place gets in your blood. Not sure how to explain it but everyone I know who's moved here, never goes back."

"That's how I feel about L.A. The energy's addictive. All the shopping, the entertainment. You can't beat it. New York's similar, but for me it can't compare to L.A. Weather's better, too."

"I see that big rock on your hand. What's your husband like?"

She stopped and looked down at the ring. She'd become so accustomed to wearing it, she'd forgotten she still had it on. "Thanks for reminding me." She slid it off her finger.

He appeared confused, so she explained. "My fiancé sent me a text this morning breaking off our engagement."

"A text?"

"Yep." She wanted to fling the ring into the trees, but pushed it into the pocket of her capris instead.

"That's pretty cold."

"He's going to marry a woman in his office. They're over in Tokyo. He said she was smart, spontaneous and a lot of fun. Which means I'm none of those things, I suppose." Her anger and humiliation rose again.

"Damn."

Silence grew between them for a moment and Anita found herself going back over the last couple years with Greg in an attempt to see if there were any signs she might have missed. She thought back on Cancun and wondered if she'd been played.

"You want me to fly us to Tokyo so I can kick his ass?"

She laughed and wiped at the sheen of tears in her eyes. "I'm sorry. Didn't mean to dump this on you."

"It's okay. And I meant it. I will fly you to Japan and I will kick his ass."

She met his eyes and saw a hint of anger in them. "You would, wouldn't you?"

"Oh, hell, yes. What kind of gutless jerk breaks up with a woman by text? Especially you."

Anita stilled. "But you don't know anything about me."

"Sure I do. You're frosty, gorgeous and fearless. A man doesn't need to know much more."

She didn't know how to take that, but his words were doing a lot to salve the reignited hurt and, even if he didn't mean them, they made her feel better. "Thanks for the compliment."

"You're welcome."

They started off again, Anita's thin-soled sandals were now so wet her feet were sliding around as if they were coated with olive oil. She ignored it as much as she could. "What about you? Married?"

"Nope. Not likely to be, either."

"Why not?"

He shrugged. "Too solitary. Too laid-back. Too selfish to want my wings clipped by a nine-to-five, or a mortgage. I like my life the way it is. I fly my chopper. I hike through places like this, and occasionally ride a board."

"You surf?"

"Learned as soon as I moved here. Part of that jarhead thing, I think."

She nodded understandingly. In spite of their conversation, she still knew next to nothing about him, but what little he'd revealed made her want to know more. "Suppose you decided to marry someone from say, Wisconsin, and she wanted you to move there. Would that be a deal breaker?"

"More than likely."

"Really?"

"Sure. Knowing I don't want to live any other place but here means the marriage probably wouldn't last very long."

"Makes sense, I suppose."

Once again, their gazes lingered and she felt a call inside that she'd never heard before.

They pressed on. Every now and then she glanced over to see how he and his bad knee were doing and each time he looked at her, she found it harder and harder to break the contact. She'd never been with a man who affected her the way he did and she had no idea what to do about it, or if she wanted to. Next to Greg, Steve Blair was as wild and untamed as the island he cared for so much.

Thoughts of Greg made her wonder what he'd've done had he been stuck in a helicopter. It went without saying he wouldn't've had a jarhead solution nor would he have asked her to make a forty-foot jump into his arms. He functioned well in the world of cocktail parties, judicial settings and black-tie events but out here in the wide-open spaces of Kauai, he'd be as out of his element as she was. To be fair, comparing the two men was like comparing apples to oranges; Blair seemed honorable. Greg was not.

Steve was doing his best not to come on to her. As he'd noted back at the hangar in L.A., he didn't do high-class, executive types, but for some reason, she was getting past his barriers. He didn't know what it was about her that had him going against his principles. At first glance, she was everything he didn't like, but he'd been impressed by how she'd met the challenges they'd faced today and how she seemed to be holding up over being betrayed. He still found her story of being dumped by her fiancé unbelievable. Outwardly she appeared to be handling that well, too. Didn't her ex appreciate the steel beneath all that glamour and attitude? Being the son of a strong Southern woman, Steve respected and admired female strength so he was thankful Anita wasn't one of those weak, sniveling types. From a strictly male perspective, her lean toned body was a plus, too, but her backbone and courage was the icing on the cake.

Steve was also doing his best to keep pace. Even though they were moving slow, his knee was fighting him all the way. Had he not been injured, they'd've already made it to Ferg's place. Instead, he was hobbling along like an old man and the marine in him hated it. Knights in shining armor weren't supposed to limp. He glanced over at his companion. She looked whipped. He could see her trying to warm herself against the damp chill by rubbing her hands up and down her bare arms, but he knew it wasn't helping much. He'd've offered her the shirt tied around his waist, but it was as damp and wet as the rest of him. After she returned home to L.A., she'd probably never want to return to the islands again, and that would be too bad, because there was so much more he wanted her to see. "Think you'll ever come back here once you get home to L.A.?"

"Nope. Not going to lie. I can't wait to leave this place."

"That's too bad. There's still a lot I'd like to show you."

Anita slowed and stopped. "Like what?"

"The sunsets at Polihale Beach, the whales and seals at Port Allen. The thousand-foot cliffs overlooking the water at Na Pali. The lagoon at Wailua River where we'd go snorkeling."

The tone of his voice and the intensity in his gaze had her heart racing.

"I'd even teach you to surf."

Once again, she found herself overwhelmed by his larger-than-life presence. Everything about him was so tantalizing and seductive, she bet very few women told him no. In an effort to save herself from succumbing to the spell he seemed to be weaving, she tossed back as nonchalantly as she could, "Are you hitting on me, Blair?"

"I think so, but I'm blaming it on the pain and the concussion."

She shook her head and smiled.

"How long were you engaged to the dummy?"

"A year, but we started dating when I was in high school."

"That's a long time."

"Yes, it is, especially when it ends up like this."

"Did you love him?"

She shrugged. "Yes, I guess. There weren't any sparks or fireworks like in one of those romance novels but I was okay with it."

"Wrong answer."

She stopped. "What do you mean, wrong answer?"

"I'm no expert on love but, judging by my parents and the marriages of my aunts and uncles, there's supposed to be fireworks and sparks. My folks are in their sixties and they can't keep their hands off each other. Embarrassed me to no end when I was in my teens and I'd walk in the kitchen to find them kissing. Yes, if I ever do get married, that's what I'll be looking for."

"Real life isn't a romance novel."

"Tell my parents that and, if I had been your fiancé, the wedding would've taken place the day after I put that big fat rock on your hand."

She felt as though she was drowning. All she could manage in response was, "That's not how it works."

"Maybe in your world, Counselor."

"Can we change the subject?"

"Sure."

"Thank you, Mr. Blair."

"My pleasure."

There was that word again. *Pleasure.* For an unguarded

moment, she found herself wondering how he might put the word into action. Appalled at the turn in her thoughts, she ignored them or at least tried to and set out walking again. It occurred to her that her growing attraction to him might be shock. After all, in addition to Greg's email, she'd been in a helicopter crash and she'd bumped her head. Were she in her right mind, she'd be running from him like her panties were on fire—one, he'd didn't have a proper job and apparently no aspirations to secure one; two, he was content to spend his days flying, hiking and occasionally surfing; and three, he needed a shave.

If she were to bring him home to meet her folks, her father would die of happiness and her mother would faint away like an old-school movie heroine. Yet and still, she found herself unable to stop taking peeks at the cut of his beard-shrouded jaw, the strength in his build and the lines of his bare arms and shoulders in the thin sleeveless tank. Add to that the camouflage pants and boots, and even with the crutch, he looked like a man of action and purpose; one perfectly capable of catching a woman jumping from a tree at forty feet. A female of lesser morals would've already stripped and offered herself to him just to get a taste of that. Appalled again, she prayed they'd get to the cabin soon, because yes, she'd lost her mind.

Steve wondered how she really felt about her fiancé's text. He assumed she still had feelings for the man. Would his text keep her from looking for love in the future the way his own Dear John letter from Yvette had left him gun-shy? He didn't have an answer, and since it wasn't really any of his business, and because her plan was to go back to L.A. and never return, he thought it best to put the wondering away and concentrate on reaching their destination—but looking over at her made that hard to do.

Finally, the cabin came into view. "There it is."

Anita was a bit taken aback not only by the size, but by

beauty of the place gleaming at the top of a hill. The entire front was glass, probably to take advantage of the outstanding view, and for some reason it reminded her of the house from the dream she'd had the morning she had overslept and missed the meeting at work. The roof was flat and dark. "When you said cabin, I was expecting Abraham Lincoln, not something out of *Architectural Digest.*"

"Nice, isn't it? Made of steel and glass. The entire place runs on solar power. From the stove and the washer and dryer to the flat screen."

She was impressed.

On the front of the huge steel entrance door was a relief of a large wave rising up out the sea. She swore she'd seen something similar to the image before but wasn't sure where. "Why's this drawing or whatever it is look so familiar?"

While he punched in a code in the lock beside the frame, she ran her hand over the raised lines.

"It's a copy of *The Great Wave* by Katsushika. It's pretty famous."

"But this is a metal door. How was all this etching done?"

"Welding torch."

Anita had never seen anything like it. She was impressed by the detail and beauty and that he knew the name of the work and the artist.

Inside she looked around. The silent interior could have easily belonged to any house in California. The furnishings were sparse but modern. A long hallway led to the kitchen at the back of the place where the entire wall, also glass, looked out on a cascading waterfall. Her jaw dropped. She turned back to Blair and met his grin.

"Beautiful, isn't it?"

She agreed. "It looks close enough to touch."

"The waterfall was the reason the place was built here. Took a year just to get the site cleared and another few to complete the house. Every beam, steel panel and pane of glass had to be flown in by chopper."

She glanced around at the modern kitchen but the waterfall kept drawing her eyes back to its flow. "Is he an architect?"

"In a way. His dad owns a construction company. Ferg made a lot of connections with building and tech guys when we were in the service. A lot of the cutting-edge stuff here are products being tested by the military, NASA and other agencies."

She wondered how much money had gone into the construction of the place but she was too well brought up to ask.

"Tell you what," he said. "You go look around. I'll get on the sat phone and see if I can't raise somebody at the airport. Bathroom's down that hall."

In the bathroom, Anita took one look at herself in the mirror and shuddered. With the goose egg on her forehead, her dirt-streaked face and wild hair, she could be the winner in a Halloween fright contest. But she was alive. Her headache had subsided and she was alone in the wilds of Hawaii with a man whose voice alone made her want to take off her clothes. She shook her head. Turning away from her scary face, she did a quick assessment of the bathroom and saw all the conveniences of home. The glistening black tiles in the shower's walls were reminiscent of the black sand she'd viewed near Kilauea. She dearly wanted to jump into it and get clean, but she needed to ask Blair if his absent friend might mind first.

She found him outside talking on a phone hooked up to a contraption that looked like a flat square piece of beige plastic.

"Damn!" she heard him say into the headset. "Okay. Good to know. I'll call back in the morning."

She wondered why he looked so grim. "What's up?"

He ran a hand over his face. He looked as bone weary as

she had in the mirror. "Apparently the storm that made us crash, also hit Lihue. The airport's shut down."

"Oh, no."

"Wind blew around everything not tied down—small planes, choppers."

It was as if the gods were conspiring to keep her on the island. "What about the resort?"

"Extensive damage. Phones and electricity out for now."

"Wow," she said softly. "I need to call my parents. Can I use that?"

"Sure, here."

He handed off the headset and showed her how to dial.

"What's this big square thing?" she asked.

"Antenna. I'm going to hobble inside. Be back in a few, talk as long as you need to."

Watching him grimace as he moved made her concern rise. She wondered if he was more injured than he'd admitted.

She called her father and the first thing he asked was how she was handling the breakup with Greg. "I'm okay. It's not every day you get dumped by text."

"He did it by text!" he yelled. "He didn't have the balls to tell you to your face? What the hell's the matter with him?"

She really didn't want to talk about this but had no choice. "I don't know, Daddy."

She let him rant and rave for a few more moments before cutting in. "The tour helicopter I was in this morning crashed."

"What!"

After telling him about the chopper crash and how she lost her phone, she repeatedly assured him that she was okay. Over the next ten minutes, she answered all of his questions about where she was, the identity of the pilot and whether she was worried about being alone with him. Truthfully, she was, but not in the sense her father meant, and of course she kept that to herself. They also discussed the storm's effects on the airport and resort, and how soon she might be able to make it back to civilization. She gave him her best estimate based on what Blair had learned from talking to the airport people. Her father wasn't pleased with the non-definitive answer, forcing her to assure him yet again that she was safe and would remain so.

"Will you call Mom and tell her about the crash and that I'm okay?" For Diane, news of the crash would be secondary. Her main focus would be the breakup with Greg. Anita was sure she'd be accused of being the cause behind his decision and she was in no mood to try and convince her mother otherwise.

"I'll call her and I expect you to call me at least twice a day until you get back to the resort so I'll know you're okay."

"I will."

"Promise me."

"I promise."

"Holding you to that, baby girl."

They spoke for a few more minutes and she ended the call.

Sitting in the silence afterward, she was suddenly overcome by how much Greg and then the crash had taken out of her. As a result, she was so morose, she wanted to have a pity party, but knowing that would only make things worse, she shook it off, pulled herself together and went inside.

Chapter 8

He had the nerve to be coming down the hall with a towel wrapped around his bare waist and another in his hand he was using to dry his hair. He'd taken a shower! But Anita's shock played second fiddle to the sight of his glistening-clean gladiator body. She'd already been mesmerized by the sculpted arms and shoulders. This was her first look at his lean, powerful legs. He was so gorgeously made he left her breathless.

"You talk to your parents?"

Anita realized she'd been staring and from the knowing look on his face, he knew it, too.

"Uhm, yes. Talked to my dad. He's going to call my mom and maybe hire a hit man to take care of Greg."

"I like your dad. Help yourself to the shower. Water should be still hot."

The thought of basking in hot water until she was clean again was like being told she'd just hit the California lottery. "Your friend wouldn't have any female clothing around that

I can put on when I'm done, would he? These are shot." She looked down at the stained and no longer white capris.

"No female clothing for sure, but go wash up and I'll see what I can find. You can toss your stuff into the washer later if you like."

Nodding her thanks and trying not to think about the effects the gladiator body was having on her senses, she slipped by him and hurried down the hall.

Making use of the available shampoo and soap, she showered quickly because she didn't know how long the hot water would last. When she was done, she swore she'd never felt so clean. She dried off with the clean towel apparently left by him for her on a hook on the door and when she finished, she wrapped it around herself before leaving the steam-filled room.

Steve, wearing a clean tank and shorts borrowed from Ferg's closet, was seated at the kitchen table winding a long bandage around his bum knee when she returned. Wrapped in the towel with her arms and legs bare, she looked fresh as morning dew. Hot, too. At the sight of her, his body reacted in typical male fashion and he was glad to be sitting down so the evidence of his desire stayed hidden. The thought that it wouldn't take more than a slight tug on the towel to let him feast on her in a slow unhurried fashion added to the hardness between his thighs. Refocusing his attention on wrapping his knee, he asked without looking up, "How was the shower?"

"Wonderful. How's your knee?"

"Be better after I get it wrapped. Headache's mostly gone, too."

"So's mine. Wish I could say the same thing about this ostrich egg on my forehead."

He gave the lump a visual assessment. "Makes you look very Klingon-ish."

Anita rolled her eyes. "Did you find me some clothes?"

"A T-shirt and some shorts that'll be way too big, but I found a tie you can use for a belt. They're in the bedroom on the bed."

"Thanks." The quiet intensity in his gaze hypnotized her so thoroughly and so well, she couldn't move and admittedly, didn't want to.

He asked softly, "You hungry?"

She was, but for more than food. The erotic thought shook her because she'd never considered herself to be that kind of woman before. "Are you cooking?"

He didn't respond at first, but the heat flowing between them didn't need words. "I can, if that's what you want. You know we're talking about more than food. Right, Counselor?"

"I do."

She watched him rise to his feet and walk to where she stood. Looking up into his burning gaze, she admitted softly, "I've never done anything like this before…I mean with someone I barely know."

A small smile crept free. "Just think of it as part of the adventure." He reached up and traced a finger over her lips. She felt herself shaking.

"If this isn't what you want, just say so," he whispered. "Yes, I'll be disappointed but I'd never force you into something you don't want to do."

He bent and slid a kiss over her earlobe. "But know this, if it is what you want, I plan to make love to you in every room in this house, Counselor. Outside, too."

Anita almost came then and there. His lips were meandering slowly over the side of her throat and jawline. The small sparks of desire they kindled and left in their wake made her close her eyes and remind herself to breathe.

"So, yes, or no?"

Her knees were weak as butter and her will, gone. She'd only been with one man in her life. Greg. And he had never started their lovemaking this way. Blair's slow lingering kisses coaxed her senses into life gently, sweetly. He seemed to be inviting her, wooing her, letting her bloom and warm herself like a sunflower in the sunshine. Greg had always seemed to be in a rush to get her undressed and into bed. He'd never taken the time to bring her to ready like this wild man of Kauai seemed intent upon doing and, as a result, she was more ready than she'd ever been before. His traveling hands were equally languid. The tail of the towel around her body was moving scandalously over the under curve of her hip. She felt the heat from his hand singeing her skin.

Steve wanted to touch and taste every inch of her. Concentrating for the moment on her sassy mouth, he teased his tongue over the corner of her lips until she took it in and let him savor the sweetness within. His hand moving the towel over her equally sassy behind slid beneath to make contact with her still-damp skin and his manhood tightened appreciatively. He could kiss her until the end of time and it would never be enough. The initial shyness he had sensed in her at the outset had given way to willing participation. Her soft gasps, the way she purred when his hand captured the soft weight of her hips—and offered him the small hollow of her throat so he could place hot flicks from the tip of his tongue against it—added more fire to his growing need.

Anita didn't know lovemaking could be this overwhelming. She didn't remember losing her hold on the towel, but at some point she must have because it was pooled at her feet. His mouth on her breasts filled her with such soaring sensations, small groans of pleasure rose in the silent kitchen. His mouth was magical; his hands lyrical. Every cell in her body was alive and preening from his touch. She didn't care that she knew so little about him she didn't even know his age, but she didn't want his loving to stop.

"Let's head to the bedroom," he murmured against her ear

while his fingers dallied with the temple between her thighs. "First time shouldn't be on the floor or a table—which may happen if we don't."

But his touches were so fiery and her body so primed, she couldn't stop the orgasm that broke and slowly rippled through her like a coursing waterfall. Riding the languid rhythm of his continued coaxing, she moaned and sagged against his strong chest to keep body and soul together and to keep from melting like honey to the floor.

Like the gladiator he was, he picked her up. Through the pulsing haze that had become her world, she sensed herself moving and then they were in the bedroom and she was supine and once again under his bewitching spell.

"I need to find a condom," he whispered. "Don't move. Be right back."

She couldn't have moved if Jane suddenly appeared in the room with partnership papers in hand for her to sign. She felt sleek, feminine and wondered if this was what he meant by sparks.

A moment later, he returned, and as he worshipped her body like the supplicant of a carnal goddess, she purred and preened, gasped and groaned. Nothing in life prepared her for the thorough loving he gave her, so when he entered and filled her, she orgasmed again.

Pleased by her sweet cries of completion, Steve pleasured her hot lithe body with a slow, steady measure. She was so tight and wet, he wanted to go all-out. Forcing down the orgasm hovering on the edges of his consciousness from the moment he had touched her, he wanted to take as much time with her as his body would allow. Thrusting, he reached possessively for her breasts and brought down his mouth to make sure the nipples stayed tight and ripe. She twisted sinuously, meeting him stroke for stroke, and was more deliciously responsive than he'd ever imagined. His body refused to wait any longer, however. Increasing his pace, he grabbed her hips roughly. The orgasm filled him and when it broke, his hips and thrusting increased to light speed. He threw back his head and growled soundlessly before collapsing, spent.

Moments later their eyes met. He wasn't sure what he expected to see but it certainly wasn't shyness. He kissed her softly and withdrew. For a moment they lay on their backs, their breaths floating in the silence of the bedroom.

"You know what's funny?" she asked.

He turned his head. "What?"

"I never knew it could be so—*good,* I guess is the word, I'm looking for."

"Really?"

"I'm serious. I always thought sex was just a man thing."

Steve did his best to keep a straight face while enjoying her wondrous tone. "Never had a man pleasure you beforehand?"

She shook her head.

"Since it's real rude to knock another man's technique, let's just say—sorry to hear that."

"Is this what you meant by sparks?"

"Yes."

She met his gaze for the first time. "Thank you."

"Not sure what you're thanking me for, but you're welcome."

"I'm thanking you for keeping me from going through the rest of my life not knowing there could be more than just—you know."

"More than just *wham bam, thank you, ma'am.*"

"Yes," she responded with a quiet chuckle in her voice.

"Glad you enjoyed yourself."

She had, but Anita was unsure what to make of it. She was the only child of high-powered parents; she'd grown up privileged, been a debutante, graduated from Stanford Law and saw the world as her oyster. She was smart and considered herself quite worldly. All her life, she'd viewed the physical act of being with a man as something to be tolerated; a view encouraged by her mother during the few talks they'd had while Anita was growing up. Men were men, and women were supposed to accommodate them. Good girls certainly never enjoyed themselves. Of course, Anita had seen movies and read books where that wasn't the case, but she'd chalked it up to them being themselves, which had nothing to do with her. Lovemaking with Greg certainly hadn't altered her thinking. However, Steve Blair turned her world upside down. Every inch of her body was primed. Just looking at him made her nipples tighten with the memory of his licks and sucking. Her mouth felt swollen and ripe. The spot between her thighs was thick and wet and she didn't know if her hips would ever let go of the feel of him moving hard and fast within. If she thought she was out of her element after the copter crash, she was in another galaxy this time around. "I'm really out of my element here, Blair."

He appeared amused. "Why?"

The magical touch of his finger whispering a slow circle around the circumference of her nipple made her mind go blank and her lids slid closed. Whatever she was going to say vanished. His tongue replaced the finger, mimicking the lazy arousal, and her hips rejoiced.

"You were saying?" he murmured while treating her other nipple to the same splendid torture. His hand strayed down between her thighs. "You're very wet, Counselor."

As if responding to a secret command, her legs opened farther. He raised his lips to her ear. "Ever had a man want you again and again?" Two long-boned fingers eased into her heat and her whole body caught fire like a flare.

"No," she breathed. In the past, it was always one and done.

"Do you want more?" He treated her to a languid erotic

rhythm that soon had her moving in tandem with the scandalous ins and outs of his fingers.

"Yes." Arching, she fed sensually. For a woman who'd always been conscious of how she had presented herself, Anita didn't care how she looked. He could make her walk naked on the L.A. freeways as long as he continued his delicious seductiveness. Another orgasm rose, gaining strength in response to the sheer bliss. From the nipples he was now pleasuring to the fingers she was riding so greedily, she'd become formless sensation. That he planned to love her again sent her soaring higher.

He left her for a breathless moment to put on another condom, then entered her again, hard and hot. Her orgasm exploded and she cried out once more from the force and magnitude. Aftershocks rocked her while he stroked and filled his hands with her hips to raise her to his liking. It was primal, raw and oh so glorious. She came again, this time on the heels of his own yelled completion, then they melted bonelessly onto the tangled sheets of the bed.

When they were able to breathe again, he kissed her deeply. "Come shower with me."

He must've seen the surprise in her eyes. "No?"

Anita had no idea how to explain, to this larger-than-life man, that showering with a guy was yet another thing out of her realm. In the past, Greg took his shower and she took hers.

"Something else new, Counselor?"

"Yes."

"For such a high-powered lady, you have led a very sheltered life."

Her embarrassment showed.

"Tell you what," he said, stroking her cheek softly. "When you head back to L.A., you can resume your regularly scheduled programming but, while we're together, I'm going to treat you to every hedonistic joy I can come up with."

"You're a mess. You know that, right?"

"Lady, you ain't seen nothing yet."

And with that, he scooped her off the bed and carried her laughing out of the room.

For the second time that day, Anita found herself in the black-tiled shower but this time she wasn't washing off the dirt and grime of the crash, nor was she alone. To her delight, Captain Steve Blair wasn't done with her. It began with his warm soapy hands traveling over her water-slick skin. Any misgivings she might have had about the appropriateness of this activity soon fled as her senses awakened once more.

Steve couldn't believe he wanted this woman again, but he did. The feel of her skin beneath his hands, the way she purred under his touch were arousing as hell. In spite of her high-profile, twenty-first-century ways, she was as green as a seventeenth century virgin bride when it came to lovemaking. Just thinking about all the passion he wanted to introduce her to made him hard as a steel beam.

Once they were both clean, he eased up behind her until their bodies were flush so he could reacquaint himself to the soft weight of her breasts, the tightened tips of her nipples and the dampness between her thighs. "Put your hands on the wall, baby," he whispered, lips against her ear. She braced herself and he slid his shaft in from behind. She groaned sensually, and as she took him in, the tight seal of their joining made him swear he'd died and gone to heaven.

"Oh, my," she moaned softly.

He sensed that this, too, was new to her. "Just hold on and let me do the work."

And work her he did; slowly at first in order for her to learn the rhythm. Moments later, she began responding, enticing him with the controlled movements of her sassy behind against his thighs. Pleased, he increased the pace until he was rocking her hard and she was gasping and crooning and twisting. Orgasm shattered her and then him, and together they fell silently against the shower wall under the now-tepid spray.

Anita's legs were rubber by the time he wrapped her in a clean towel and carried her back into the bedroom. She had no idea what he had in store next but she was sure it was going to take her some time to find the pieces of herself to put back together again.

"Still enjoying yourself?" he asked.

"Immensely."

He set her on the edge of the bed. "How about I cook us something to eat?"

She'd totally forgotten that the subject of food was how this whole passion-filled interlude had begun.

"First though, I need you to put on some clothes."

She looked down at the towel wrapped around herself then up into his still-burning gaze. Fueled by all they'd been doing and how female she felt, she slowly undid the towel and let it drop. "I thought this was supposed to be a hedonistic adventure."

He grinned. "It is, but if I tip your sexy little butt back onto that bed, it'll be midnight before we come up for air, and we'll starve to death, so get dressed."

"Party pooper," she pouted.

Next she knew he was kissing her and slowly running heat-inducing hands over her clean damp skin. Her body began responding to his call. His mouth found her nipples. His fingers the tiny citadel at the apex of her thighs. He didn't turn her loose until she saw stars. How kisses could be so overpowering she had no idea.

"Will that hold you for a while, Counselor?"

Reeling, she whispered, "Yes."

"Good." Giving her a long parting kiss and then a grin, he left the room.

* * *

Wearing an oversize white tee and a pair of black shorts held up by a bright red tie, the thoroughly loved and barefoot Anita sat at the kitchen table watching him as he fried up bacon and cracked eggs into a bowl for omelets. As he chopped veggies and went back to the fridge for cheese, it was pretty obvious that he was as familiar with cooking as he was with a woman's body, which was good because she couldn't boil water. What other secrets did he hold? she wondered, and why did the thought of leaving him and this paradise in a few days suddenly feel so wrong.

A potential partnership with Sheridan Law awaited her return to L.A., a partnership she'd craved with every beat of her heart for three years. But now, her heart seemed to be beating to a new and different drum and, no matter how much she wanted to ignore it, the cadence kept gaining force. His lovemaking was responsible for much of the beat. He'd turned her inside out, and all she could think about was *more*. In less than the time it took to sign a merger agreement, she'd gone from the staid and conservative Anita Hunt to a woman whose well-ordered life path had been sensually hijacked by a man she'd met—what?—two days ago.

He was so outside of what she'd imagined a man in her life would be that she was having trouble distinguishing up from down. She didn't even know how much money he made, who his parents were or where he'd gone to school. Parts of her wondered if she'd gone crazy but, when he glanced her way, his smile warmed her so much, she willingly embraced crazy because it felt so good. "You know your way around this kitchen pretty well."

"Up here a lot. Ferg likes to cook, too. During football season we make these huge meals then take my dog out for a run to work it all off."

"You have a dog?"

"Yep. Rottweiler named Dog."

She laughed. "The dog's name is Dog?"

"You have a problem with that?" he asked with humor in his voice.

He folded the omelet in the skillet with an expertise she also found impressive. "How long have you had him?"

"Four years. He originally belonged to a friend of mine who died over in Baghdad."

Although he masked it well, she got the sense that the story was a sad one. "Didn't mean to bring up bad memories."

"You're good." He told her about the promise he'd made to David Tanaka about taking the then pup to Mrs. T if anything happened. "When I escorted the puppy and David's casket home, I fell in love with the island so much that, at the end of my tour, instead of going home to Texas, I came here and stayed. I live in a little house behind his mom's."

She wondered what his home looked like and if it was as laid-back, as easygoing, as him. "Your parents were okay with you not coming home?"

He shrugged while bringing the plates to the table. "I was grown. My life. My choice. They knew it had nothing to do with not loving them. I needed time to put myself back together again after Iraq. Mentally."

He was probably the first combat soldier she'd ever spoken with and it came to her that there were a lot more levels to Steve Blair than she'd realized. "How many tours did you do?"

"Two. Had planned to be a lifer, but I found out I didn't like death—not causing it, seeing it—or burying friends as a result of it."

"Did you lose many?"

"Yeah."

She saw the pain and weariness show itself in his eyes.

"Let's eat," he said softly.

Chapter 9

They ate their omelets outside at a small picnic table positioned to enjoy the view of the canyon's magnificent waterfall. Steve watched her surreptitiously and wondered what she might be thinking. He didn't usually allow people past his barriers, especially those he didn't know, but he had with her. He wasn't naive enough to believe her interlude here with him would be anything more than a fond memory for her down the road, but parts of him wanted it to be more.

For the first time since Yvette's Dear John letter, he found himself with a woman he honestly wanted to get to know. He'd already admitted being attracted to the steel hiding beneath the silken exterior, but he also found himself wanting to explore her complexities. On one hand she was the frosty, big-money lawyer: confident, smart, blunt and on the way to the partnership she'd told him about. But as he'd noted before, in bed, she was virgin green and that drew him, too. Helping her realize just how sensual she was underneath all the frost was a job he wouldn't mind having.

But her life was in L.A. and his was in Kauai. Steve's brother, Kyle, often jokingly referred to Steve as his slacker big brother, but Kyle had spent his twenties on Wall Street wearing five-hundred-dollar suits and imported Italian shoes. Steve, on the other hand, had spent his in military fatigues dodging weapons fire while dropping soldiers into war zones, and ferrying some of those same soldiers back to base in body bags. He'd been blessed to come home whole and because he'd seen so much death, he viewed life as a gift and far too precious to spend it cooped up inside a building doing a nine-to-five while the years slipped by like sand in an hour glass.

He chose to spend his life enjoying it and because of that, it was understood he'd not be Anita's choice of a life partner; he didn't fit the mold and he was okay with that, but he wanted more time with her than the present circumstances would probably allow.

"So, what's next?" she asked pushing aside her clean plate. "Great omelet by the way."

"Thanks. My mom taught my brother and me to cook when were probably nine or ten. Said she didn't want her sons growing up not knowing how to feed themselves."

"Go, Mom," she said. "I never learned to cook."

"Why not?"

"My mother's a judge. She didn't have time to make dinner so, we always had help."

"A judge. And your daddy's in entertainment. So you're a spoiled little rich girl."

"Yes and proud to be," she tossed back smiling.

They were enjoying the camaraderie they'd forged. Reality would step in soon and send them back to their separate worlds but, for the moment, they were content to be in their secluded world and fill whatever time remained with each other's company.

"How about we take these plates back inside, clean up the kitchen, maybe go for a walk?"

"I'd love that, but—" she showed him her bare feet "—no shoes. The spoiled little rich girl's pricey sandals are over there drying in the sun. Word's still out on whether they'll survive or not."

"Then how about after we clean up we do popcorn and a movie?"

"What're we watching?"

"A favorite of mine. It's called the Heavens."

Her confusion must've shown on her face.

"You'll love it. I promise." He then asked, eyebrow raised, "You do know how to wash dishes, don't you?"

She stuck out her tongue.

"I'll wash, you dry."

The work didn't take much time and they spent most of it directing quiet smiles at each other. Anita noted how relaxed she felt being with him and reflected on the sadness he'd let her see. She got the impression that it wasn't something he revealed often. Because such things hadn't mattered to her before, she didn't know the length of a military tour of duty, nor could she imagine spending even an hour in a war zone, let alone months or years at a time. The servicemen and women putting their lives on the line so that freedom could ring never held a personal connection for her until Steve Blair. Now, a part of her wanted to heal the pain she'd witnessed in his eyes and soothe the sorrow he was carrying in his heart but she had no idea how to go about it. Once again, she was out of her element.

He made the popcorn in a standard air popper, and after pouring the fat white kernels into a large green plastic bowl, he added melted butter and shook in a little salt. He held out the bowl for her to grab some then he did the same.

"Perfect," she declared.

"Then follow me."

Outside the sun was setting in a ball of fire. The sheer beauty of it was so mesmerizing it took her breath away.

"Gorgeous, isn't it?" Steve asked. He thought she was pretty gorgeous, too, but kept that to himself. "You should see it setting over the ocean."

"It can't be more beautiful than this."

"Believe it or not, it is."

She shook her head as if finding that hard to believe. "And it sets this way every night?"

"Most of the time."

"We can't see the sun like this in L.A."

"No kidding," he teased.

"Hater."

He chuckled. "Here, hold the popcorn. I need to grab some seating."

He returned with two large sleeping bags and spread them out on the ground, one on top of the other. He sat. "Join me, Counselor."

She did and set the bowl between them. "So where's the screen, and what did you say the movie was again?"

He reached out and urged her closer. Once she was against his side, he gave her a kiss on her forehead. "The Heavens. Be on soon as it gets dark enough."

She assessed him. "Are we watching the stars? Is that what you mean by Heavens?"

"I can tell you have a trained deductive mind."

She punched him playfully and said skeptically, "We're going to sit out here, in the dark and look at the sky?"

He reached into the bowl. "And eat popcorn. Don't forget that part."

"I need to get you a Game Boy, Mr. Sky Pilot."

"You obviously need distracting if all you're going to do is talk through the opening credits. Come here...."

He pulled her onto his lap and her laugh was cut short by the slow infectious kisses he distracted her with. "I got your Game Boy," he whispered.

Anita didn't know how she wound up lying on her back with him leaning over her because she was too distracted by the lips moving gently over hers, the fiery tip of his tongue tasting hers and the hand moving possessively over her breasts in the thin white tee. She kissed him back, tempting him with her tongue, trying to brand him the way he'd branded her, and then his lips were gone, her T-shirt pulled aside momentarily so his mouth replaced the hand on her breast. She groaned, her hips rose and her back bowed. "You are so damn good at this," she whispered.

"Glad you approve. It gets better."

And angels help her, it did. He had her so hot and bothered, she didn't care when he pulled her shorts down and off. All she cared about was the bliss emanating from the wicked hand now between her thighs. He transferred his kisses to her belly and slid the hem of her shirt high on her chest so that her damp, jewel-tight nipples were as exposed to the evening as the rest of her.

"You're probably sore from earlier, so how about some of this... Spread your wings, Counselor, so your sky pilot can make you fly." His finger circled the node of flesh made specifically for a woman's pleasure and when he licked her there, she cried out in disbelief and delight.

"Like this, do you?"

Yes, indeed. It was so new, so...scandalous. She'd never had a man love her this way but soon, because he was so damn good at that, too, she lost the ability to protest or to think. The sweet ravishing had her twisting and crooning and raising herself shamelessly for more, while the oncoming orgasm rushed her like white water coming over the falls. Her cries became more vocal.

"No screaming, Counselor. You'll scare the canyon sheep."

But when he increased the intensity and gently nipped the throbbing bud, the orgasm grabbed her, shattered her into a thousand glittering pieces, and Anita screamed loud enough to scare the sheep in Saskatchewan.

Dazed and mindless, she came back to earth and knew she'd never be the same. For the rest of her life, she'd be looking for a man to sweep her away. There'd be no more settling for Anita Hunt. She now wanted sparks and fire and everything that went with it, including popcorn.

When she opened her eyes, he was smiling down. He traced her cheek and bent to give her another kiss. "Ready to watch the movie now?"

"You should be in jail, you know." The orgasm continued to reverberate.

"If I'm in jail, how will I make love to you?"

She reached up and cupped his jaw. "That would be a problem, wouldn't it?"

"I think so."

Their eyes held and the bond between them tightened and cemented. He confessed quietly, "I'm going to miss you when you go back to L.A."

"I'll miss you, too."

"Then let's watch the movie and not talk about the future." She nodded.

He settled her on his lap. She savored the feeling of being held against his heart, and watched the stars come out.

She had to admit, the show put on by the night sky was in its own way as spectacular and impressive as the Hawaiian sunset. "I don't think I've ever seen so many stars." They were like diamond dust shining overhead. He pointed out the Big and Little Dippers.

"That's Polaris, the North Star," he added. "The Hawaiian name for it is *Hokupa'a*."

"What's it mean?"

"The stationary star."

Were she home in L.A., she'd be multitasking between work and phone calls. The idea of spending any portion of the night hours watching the stars would've been laughable. Granted, once she returned home and resumed her old routine of work and more work, the idea might become laughable again, but for the present moment, this was wonderful and it made her wonder if her life should hold more experiences like this one. Without a doubt she was a changed woman but she wasn't certain who that changed woman might eventually be. As the sounds of the waterfall played like distant music, she turned her attention to the man holding her as if she were the most precious thing in this world, and knew for certain that she wanted as many experiences with him as this short interlude in paradise would allow. "Make love to me out here beneath the stars."

For Steve, it was an arousing request, and because he couldn't deny her and it was what he'd been longing to do, he replied with a kiss that left them both restless. She was already nude below the waist, so he gently placed her supine and began. He wanted this to be memorable, lasting. For the rest of her life, every time she looked up and saw the stars in the night sky, he wanted her to remember their lovemaking and yes, him. He wanted her to remember the feel of her nipples tightening like jewels in his mouth and the way his fingers opened the treasure between her thighs and plied her until she was hot and running with love. When she saw the Big Dipper, he wanted it to trigger the memory of him sliding kisses down her body and carnally worshipping her with hot flicks of his tongue while she spread her legs wide. Mostly, whenever she made love in the future, he wanted her to remember a sky pilot who turned her over and impaled her on

his rigid shaft and let her ride while he rocked her possessively until the starry sky exploded like the Fourth of July.

The next morning, Steve awakened in bed with the still-
sleeping Anita in his arms. What a night. They'd made love
until the wee hours of the morning and now, it was all coming to an end. The pilot in him could hear the distant sounds
of helicopter rotors approaching and because Ferg's place had
the only chopper pad within miles, Steve assumed whoever
was inside would be using it to land.

He roused her gently. "Wake up, darlin'. Company's coming."

Her eyes fluttered open and she smiled up at him. "Morning."

"Morning, Counselor. You should probably hit the shower
and get dressed." Steve stroked her cheek while he tried to
ignore the sadness in his heart.

She sat up and there was confusion on her face. "What?"

"I hear a chopper coming."

"Here?"

"More than likely, yes."

"Damn," she said sounding dejected. She searched his
eyes.

"I know. Go get clean. I'll meet whoever it is."

"Steve, I—"

He kissed her forehead. "No time to waste. Hurry now."

She looked like she wanted to argue but sighed and left
instead. Filled with a reluctance of his own, he pulled on his
shorts and dug out a clean tee from Ferg's dresser drawer. It
was his hope that it would be Ferg back from babysitting the
hangar in L.A., but when he stepped outside with the binoc-
ulars, he checked its markings. It belonged to one of the tour
companies from the Big Island.

The large white helicopter set itself down just as Anita
stepped outside. The sight of her parents deplaning and being

buffeted by the wings of the rotors as they hurried toward the house made her heart both rise and sink. "My parents," she told him.

She left Steve and went to greet them. Her father hugged her like he'd found treasure. "Are you okay!" he yelled.

She nodded. "What are you two doing here? Hi, Mom. Daddy, I thought you were still in Peru."

"Nope. Right after we talked, I caught a jet to Honolulu and your mother met me there. I know you said you were okay but I wanted to see for myself."

"What happened with Greg?" her mother asked. "Sylvia and I are beside ourselves."

Anita's lips tightened. "I've no idea, but let's go inside."

They entered and, before Anita could make the introductions, her mother eyed the silent Steve. "Are you the pilot who crashed with my daughter?"

"Yes, ma'am. Steve Blair. We ran into some bad weather."

"You are licensed, I assume, and you carry insurance?"

"Mother, the man saved my life. You should be thanking him."

The look on her face said no such thing would be forthcoming. Anita forced herself not to act as though she and Steve had spent the last twelve hours making mad hot love, and concentrated on making eye contact with her father.

He stepped forward, introduced himself and shook Steve's hand. "Thanks for taking care of her."

"You're welcome."

Her father then asked, "Have we met before?"

"I don't think so."

"You look familiar. Where are you from?"

"Texas."

"Blair from Texas," he echoed, thinking out loud. Then as if a lightbulb came on in his head, he pointed at Steve.

"Marcus Blair. I knew an Marcus Blair at Morehouse. Are you two related?"

Steve grinned. "That's my dad."

"I knew I knew that face! You look just like him."

"I get that a lot."

"I'll be damned. We pledged together. Haven't seen him in probably forty years. How is he?"

"Doing well."

"He still in the oil business? We used to call Marcus, O.K. for oil king. Richest kid on campus."

Steve saw Anita's surprised look. "Family's still in the business."

Her mother gave him a dismissive look and cut into the conversation. "Can we stick to why we're here, Randall?"

Still smiling, he said, "Sure, Diane. Run the show."

She turned to Anita. "I've retrieved your things from your suite at the resort. I put your change of clothes in here." She handed her a large overnight bag. "So, go get dressed, please. I'd like to return to the airport in Honolulu as soon as possible. Our flight back to L.A. is in a few hours."

Hoping her disappointment didn't show, Anita turned to Steve. "Mr. Blair, thanks so much for everything."

"You're welcome. Have a safe flight home, Ms. Hunt."

She nodded and hurried to the bedroom.

Once there, Anita changed into the long summery skirt and blouse she'd taken from the bag. Inside she also found a comb, brush and makeup. Doing what she could with her hair, she applied the makeup and viewed herself in the mirror. The knot on her forehead was still there but smaller and she was surprised her mother hadn't added that to the list of complaints. She tossed the clothes she'd removed onto the bed. Would she ever see Steve again?

Not knowing the answer added to her melancholy. Because of her parents' presence, they wouldn't be able to share any last words, and there'd definitely be no goodbye kisses. Sighing over the unfair turns her life had taken in the past few days, she picked up the bag. Before leaving however, she looked back at the bed and relived all the pleasures he'd given her there and how nice it had been to wake up with him beside her that morning. She placed the memories of their time together in her heart and walked out to rejoin her parents.

He wasn't with them.

Her dad must've seen her confusion. "Blair said he had to check the solar batteries, or something like that. I gave him my card and told him to have his dad call me."

As the pilot took the chopper and its passengers up into the air, Anita looked down at the dwindling house and prayed she'd get one last glimpse of Steve.

Her mother's voice distracted her. "Anita, tell me what happened with Greg."

"There's nothing to tell, Mother. He broke off the engagement."

When she looked down again, the house was gone.

An hour later, while Anita was boarding the jet for the return trip to L.A., Steve stood out in front of the house watching another chopper land. Ferg.

When Ferg got out, he told Steve happily, "I'm finally free."

"Welcome home. So Old Man Tate's back?"

"Yeah, but without the new young wife. Guess she ran off with a house painter in Seville. He's going to file for divorce. What's this I hear about you crashing a bird? You didn't have a passenger with you, did you?"

"Yeah, Ms. January."

"The one with the great legs and the bad attitude? You didn't kill her, did you?"

"No, but I think I'm in love."

"What!"

Steve chuckled. "Come on in. Got a story for you."

Chapter 10

Once home, Anita booted up her computer and ordered a new mobile phone and replacements for the credit cards and passport lost in the crash. That done, she sat down on the sofa and let the weariness take over. Seated next to her mother on the plane had been a nightmare. When she wasn't giving Anita the third degree about the breakup with Greg or intimating that somehow it had to have been Anita's fault, she was pressuring her to move back East to facilitate finding a new job and a replacement fiancé.

Never mind the potential partnership, it was more important to get a ring on her finger, Diane advised pointedly. Even if she divorced the mythical replacement later in life, at least she'd be able to claim she'd been married. Anita thought she might go insane. Finally her father had had enough. Leaning over from his window seat, he succinctly told Diane to shut the hell up and stop trying to micromanage Anita's life. Anita could've kissed him.

And now her thoughts shifted to Steve. She wondered

what he was doing and if he was wondering the same thing about her. Her body still held the physical memories of last night's lovemaking and she would've given anything to have had a bit more time to enjoy his company, not for just the pleasure, but for his sense of humor, his outlook on life and his popcorn.

However, their idyllic adventure in paradise was over and she was back in her own world again. Her plan was to stay home tomorrow and return to work the day after. With that in mind, she dashed off one last email to Jane to let her know about the crash and that she'd be at work in two days. Hoping that missing Steve would fade over time, she powered off the laptop, took a long hot shower and climbed into bed.

The phone rang. She grabbed the handset from the base and prayed it wasn't her mother. The display on the caller ID filled her with a surge of new energy. "Hey, sky pilot."

"Hey, Counselor. Just called to make sure you got home safe. Your dad gave me your number. Hope that was okay."

"It is. How are you?"

"Missing you."

The sound of his voice made her ache for him. "Missing you, too."

"That's good to hear. Sorry for not sticking around when you left. I'm not real good with goodbyes."

"It's okay." Anita leaned back against the pillows. "What're you doing?"

"Besides missing you?"

"Yes, besides missing me."

"Dog and I are sitting out on the porch. Going tomorrow to see about buying a new chopper, so I can get back in business."

"Were you as surprised as I was about our dads knowing each other?"

"I was. That was pretty wild."

"And I was really surprised to find out your family's in oil."

"Big-time, but it's not something I advertise."

"Obviously not."

"Hey, I want the girls to like me for me, not for my trust fund."

That amused her. "Well, I don't care about the trust, I just want your popcorn."

He laughed and the sound of it made her want to reach out and touch him. "Good to know because it's the size of Texas and gaining interest every minute of every day according to my brother, Kyle. My grandparents set it up."

"So, in reality you're a poor little rich boy."

Another chuckle from his end. "Yeah, but don't tell anyone."

Silence filled the line as if they were both trying to figure out what to say next. The silence was broken when he said softly, "Did I tell you how much I miss you?"

Her heart grew wings and soared. "Yes, but be nice to hear it again."

"I miss you, baby."

Anita hastily dashed away the tears forming in her eyes. She missed him so much, too. More than she'd ever missed anyone before. "So what do we do about this? Are you coming up to L.A. anytime soon?"

"Going to be tied up this week with the chopper shopping and I promised Ferg we'd go deep sea fishing for a few days, but tell you what?"

"What?"

"Ferg will have to wait. Soon as I get the chopper purchase done, I'll fly up to see you. That okay?"

"More than okay. Bring the popcorn."

"I'll bring everything we'll need."

"I'm holding you to that."

"Holding you is on my list, too."

Anita wondered if this is how it felt to be in love.

His voice broke into her thoughts. "I know how tired you must be, so I'll let you go. Here's my number."

"Hold on." She grabbed the pen and pad she kept by the phone and, when he recited the number, she wrote it down. "I should have a new phone by tomorrow afternoon." She gave him the cell phone number and her landline office number.

"Got it," he said. "Now get some sleep. I'll talk to you soon."

"Night, Steve."

"Night, Counselor. Stay sweet."

Floating, Anita cradled the handset and snuggled back into the bed. As she dropped off to sleep, she was still smiling.

Ferg flew Steve down to the hangar later that evening so he could pick up his Jeep and drive home. After a promise to get together in a few days, Steve watched Ferg take off again and he headed home. Anita filled his thoughts during the hour-long drive. After the short talk with her, he missed her even more. Her parents had been an interesting pair. He'd liked her father, but could've done without her mother looking down her nose at him the entire time. He planned to call his father first thing to see if he wanted to hook up with his old frat brother Randall Hunt, and smiled at how small the world was.

When he pulled up into the drive and knocked on Mrs. T's front door, she greeted him with a smile. Dog greeted him with happy barks and tried to knock him down. Later over a shared dinner of spaghetti and meatballs with Mrs. T, he filled her in on his adventure.

Mrs. T asked, "This Anita is the same woman in the stilettos you mentioned a few days ago?"

"Yes." Steve thought back on his initial meeting with Anita and how unimpressed he'd been but, being with her during and after the crash changed all that, and seemingly him, as well. "I think I want to buy a house."

Mrs. T paused with chopsticks in hand. "Are you in love, Steve?"

"Maybe."

Their smiles met. "Then I'll call a friend tomorrow. She's one of the best Realtors on the island."

"Thanks."

Mrs. T looked down at Dog lying contentedly on the floor by Steve's chair and asked, "Do you have something appropriate to wear to a wedding?"

Dog didn't answer, so she said, "I guess that's a no."

Steve chuckled and forked up more spaghetti.

Back at his place, he called his mother. First he related the details about the crash. When he finished, he told her that he was thinking of buying a house. She laughed and asked, "Who is she?"

"Who's who?"

"This woman you're buying this house for. You forget, I birthed you and, if you're buying a house, some woman must've rocked your world. So spill it. Who is she?"

Amused he complied.

She responded with, "My son the hermit and a high-powered L.A. lawyer. Interesting. Will I like her?"

"I hope so. Her father pledged with Dad at Morehouse."

"Oh, Lord. That's all this family needs, more purple and gold. Can't wait to meet her."

They spoke for a few minutes longer, and he ended the call with a promise to keep her posted.

Sitting in the silent room afterward, he rubbed Dog's head and said, "I think you'll like her, too."

Dog had no reply.

* * *

Anita was very happy to return to work. When she entered the office, her coworkers wanted to hear about the crash, so she spent a few minutes telling them as much as she thought they needed to know before heading down the hall to Jane's office to let her know she was back, but her door was closed and the lights were off.

Val was at her desk however, and on it sat a huge vase of gorgeous yellow roses. "Welcome back," Val said.

"Thanks. Jane coming in late?"

"No. She flew home to Minnesota on the red-eye. Her mom fell down some stairs last night and had to have emergency surgery. Because she's in her eighties, Jane said the doctors were pretty worried."

Anita's heart went out to her. "Has she checked in yet?"

"Not so far, but I'll let everybody know when she does."

She hoped the surgery went well. "Who sent you flowers?"

"They're not mine. They're for you."

That caught her by surprise. Hoping they might be from Steve, she dug out the card. It read: *So sorry. Greg.* Her jaw tightened. "Did I tell you Greg dumped me by text while I was in Hawaii?"

"No!"

"Yes and these are from him." Anita picked up the vase and promptly dropped them into Val's wastebasket.

Smiling at Val's stunned face, Anita said, "I'll see you at lunch."

Anita spent the morning working on the remaining items on the Bentley merger and fighting off the memories planted in her heart and mind by Steve Blair and his call. As for Greg, he could kick rocks.

Later that afternoon, her phone rang. The caller ID displayed her mother's name and Anita dearly wanted to ignore it but picked up. "Hi, Mom. What can I do for you?"

"Greg has come to his senses. Sylvia says he's changed his mind about marrying that other girl and he wants you back. Isn't that exciting?"

"No, it isn't."

"What do you mean, it isn't?"

Anita could feel a headache forming. "Greg and I are done, Mom. I'm not marrying him. He sent me flowers this morning and I threw them in the trash."

"The man made a mistake. He's admitted it. The least you can do is be gracious."

"He didn't even have the guts to dump me face-to-face. I'm not marrying a man like that."

"Oh, Anita, stop being so dramatic and listen to me. Greg is the best—"

She cut her off. "I'm late for a staff meeting. Tell Aunt Sylvia I'm sorry things didn't work out. I have to go, Mom." And she hung up.

The phone rang again. It was Diane calling back. Anita let it ring and walked over to the window and looked down on the street. After being directed to voice mail for the fifth time, her mother finally gave up and Anita walked back to her desk. She took out Steve's number. She wanted to hear his voice. As it began to ring, she smiled, but then heard a computerized voice say, "The party you are trying to reach has not set up a mailbox. Please try your call at another time."

"Who doesn't set up their mailbox!" she yelled. She reminded herself that he was the same man who called looking at the stars going to the movies, which made her smile. She missed him.

For the next few days, Anita threw herself into work and, at night, when she was alone, she thought of and dreamed of Steve: his kisses, his smile, the way he made her enjoy life. She found herself wanting to see the ocean and hear the quiet drumming of waterfalls. Driving home in the dark after yet another long day at work, she longed to see stars in the night sky but in L.A. that was impossible. Steve was correct about the island effects. As the days progressed, she missed him and Kauai more and more.

When Anita came to work that next morning, she noticed the lights on in Jane's office. "Is she back?" she asked Val.

"Yes, but her mom's not doing well. Jane said she wanted to see you first thing."

"About?"

Val's face was blank. "Just go on in, she's waiting."

Wondering what the meet might be about and dearly hoping it would be a yes on the partnership, Anita went in. The first thing she noticed was how tired her boss appeared. "Val said you wanted to see me."

"I do. Have a seat."

Anita complied. "How's your mom?"

"Not well. She's going to need long-term twenty-four hour care."

"I'm so sorry to hear that."

"She fell due to a stroke, so I'm going home to take care of her. I love her too much to turn the job over to strangers."

"I understand."

"In order to do that though, I'm going to have to dissolve the firm."

Anita couldn't hide her surprise.

"I'm sorry, Anita. I know how much you wanted the partnership. That's the bad news. The good news is this. Do you remember Mike Moran of Moran and Associates?"

"Yes. I worked with him and his group on my very first merger for you."

"Yes, you did and he sang your praises for months afterward."

"He was easy to work with and he knew his stuff."

"I've spent the last few days making calls to find other

firms to take on some of my better people and Mike wants you to come and work for him. He's agreed to give you a partnership, if you join his crew."

Anita was stunned.

"There is a catch however. Eighteen months ago, he moved his main office to Honolulu and I know you had a real bad experience in Hawaii so you might not be too keen on living there."

"When are you planning on dissolving the firm?"

"Soon as possible."

"And when would Mr. Moran want me to start?"

Jane handed her a business card with Moran's logo on it. "Soon as you can. Call him first. He wants to fly you down and talk."

Anita looked at the card while all kinds of happiness blossomed inside. Was she actually going to be able to return? "Thanks, Jane. I'll give him a call. How soon do you want us to vacate the office?"

"I'd like everyone out by the end of the week. Again, I'm sorry."

"You don't have to apologize for loving your mother. Go home and do what you need to do. We'll be fine."

"Thanks, I appreciate that and I've truly enjoyed working with you."

Anita closed the door quietly behind her exit.

Val said, "So now you know."

"Yes, I do. She found me another firm, though."

"Me, too, and it's in L.A. so I can finish school."

"That's wonderful."

Back in her office, Anita sat down in her chair and tried to determine her true feelings. On the one hand, the prospect of being in Hawaii was like a dream come true but, if it didn't work out with Moran, she faced starting the climb to partner from the bottom somewhere else. She looked at the card in her hand and picked up the phone to give Moran a call.

The call went well. He agreed to fly her to Honolulu early next week. Now, all she had to do was get in touch with her sky pilot and let him know what was going on.

Chapter 11

Anita was extremely happy when she pulled into her condo's parking space. Hawaii and Steve were on her mind. She couldn't wait to talk to him and give him the news about the Moran job, but she was brought up short by the sight of Greg Ford sitting on her front porch. Angry that he'd shown up to ruin one of the happiest days of her life, she asked coldly, "What do you want?"

"How are you?"

"What the hell do you want, Greg?"

"Just a chance to talk."

"You have two minutes." She glanced at her watch. "Starting now."

"Uhm. Well. I'm here to eat humble pie."

"Not necessary."

He looked visibly relieved. "Your mother said if I give you a few days to cool off you'd come to your senses."

"You think I said 'not necessary' because I'm taking you back?"

He looked wary. "Well, yes."

"Are you doing crack these days?"

He jumped. "Anita!"

"Go to hell. You didn't have the balls to tell me to my face."

"But that's why I'm here. I'm ashamed of how I treated you and I'd like to apologize."

"Then do it and go."

"Will you at least have dinner with me, for old times' sake?"

"No."

"Please, Anita. If we can't resolve this over dinner, I promise to never bother you again."

"Fine. I'll be ready in an hour."

She brushed by him and put her key in the door. When he tried to come in, she told him, "Wait in your car."

His eyes went wide. She stepped inside and closed the door.

In an hour she was ready. She made a point to put on the slinkiest designer gown in her closet: a midnight-blue number that hugged her curves like the fins of a mermaid. Her makeup and hair were fierce and so was her jewelry. She wanted to show him what he'd thrown away.

When she stepped outside his mouth dropped. "Wow."

"Where's your car. Let's go."

He tried to make conversation on the way but she was having none of it and by the time they reached Zola's of all places, he'd gone silent.

"Why here?" she asked.

"Your dad suggested it."

"My dad?"

"Yes, I talked to him. He's going to join us."

Anita stared. What in the world was her father thinking? Was he on Greg's side after all? Stunned, she waited for the valet to open her door before she stepped out.

Inside the restaurant, she nodded a hello to Mr. Zola who

nodded in response, but she noted the very frigid stare he gave Greg as he escorted them to one of the private rooms in the rear of the restaurant. Seated at the table was her mother, Greg's mother, Sylvia, and the Judas formerly known as her father.

Her mother gushed. "See, Greg, I knew she'd come. You look stunning, dear."

"Hello, everyone," Anita said, sitting on the edge of her chair.

She shot her father a tart look but he simply smiled and raised his champagne flute in a toast. She swore she saw mischief twinkling in his eyes. She turned away and glared at Greg. The smile on his face looked as fake as she knew him to be.

Diane said, "Now that we're all here. I'd like to propose a toast to the future marriage of Greg and Anita."

Anita didn't move.

Her mother said testily, "Anita, you're supposed to raise your flute."

"I'm not marrying him, Mom, so move on."

She saw her father smile.

"Anita, listen to me—"

"Nope. Aunt Sylvia, pardon me for saying this, but your son is a ball-less wonder and I refuse to be married to him. Is that plain enough for everybody. Daddy?"

"Works for me, baby girl."

Her mother blanched and Sylvia appeared ready to faint.

"Thank you. Now that that's straight, I'm leaving." Anita stood. She was absolutely furious with her mother for her machinations.

Her father said, "Hector will call you a car to take you home."

The anger on her mother's face was plain, but it was nothing compared to the heartache Anita felt knowing that her mother would never be her champion. "Have a good evening."

And she walked out.

She found Mr. Zola at the front of the restaurant by the entrance. "My father said you'd call me a car to take me home."

"Already outside."

"Thanks."

He held open the door and pointed. "Car's over there."

Seeing Steve Blair dressed in a tux and seated behind the wheel of a sleek black convertible import made her jaw drop.

Mr. Zola smiled. "Have a good evening, Anita."

Speechless, she walked over, opened the door and got in. "What're you doing here?" She felt like a giggly teenager.

"Your father invited me to what he said was your surprise birthday party."

"He lied. My birthday's in February."

He laughed. "I'll remember that in the future. So how are you?"

"Wonderful now. Thanks for rescuing me again."

"My pleasure."

A smile warmed her insides.

"So, no party?"

"No, just my mother trying to get me to take Greg back. You look good in that tux, by the way."

"Thanks. "I thought Greg was going to marry his work buddy."

"Changed his mind."

"Of course. Like the dress. Very hot, Counselor."

"Thanks." She couldn't believe they were actually together again. "I told Greg's mom he was a ball-less wonder."

Steve snorted. "I like that, too."

"So did my dad."

"So, what else have you been doing besides pissing people off? Did you get the partnership?"

"No, in fact Jane's closing down the agency."

He turned to her. "What?"

"Yes." She explained about Jane's mother.

"So what are you going to do?"

"Move to Hawaii, looks like."

The surprise on his face made her grin, then she explained that whole scenario, as well.

"Good thing I bought a house."

Her turn to be surprised. "You bought a house?"

He nodded. "Figured we'd need one."

"So when can I see it?"

"Whenever you fly down."

"Can we go now?"

"Jet's fueled up and waiting at the airport. We can be home in nothing flat."

"Give me a few minutes to pack and I'll be ready."

"First things first. Hold out your hand. Gotta put a ring on it." Her reaction made him say teasingly, "Close your mouth, Counselor, and hold out your hand. Unless you don't want it, of course."

Anita began to cry and placed her hand over her mouth in wonder and joy.

In a voice that really made her tears flow, he asked, "Will you marry me, Anita Hunt, so we can watch sunsets and eat popcorn?"

She was so moved and so speechless, all she could do was nod.

He took a small black velvet box out of his coat and opened it. He gently took her hand and pushed the sparkler onto the third finger of her left hand. "I figured no sense in getting an engagement ring since I plan to marry you just as soon as we get all the legal stuff out the way."

Through her happy tears, she stared down at the serious rock on her finger. "This is gorgeous."

"Trust fund money does come in handy sometimes. Now, do I get my kiss?"

She threw herself at him and lost herself in the arms and kisses of the man she planned to watch sunsets with for the rest of her life.

Someone cleared their throat close by. A hazy Anita looked up to see her smiling father standing next to the car.

"So, you two good here?"

"Yes, Dad."

"Yes, Mr. Hunt."

"Then I'm good, too. Call me when you come up for air."

With that he walked away.

Steve met her shining eyes and slowly traced her mouth. "I think we should leave in the morning." The finger languidly slid down her throat and toyed with the tops of her breasts peeking up above the neckline of her fancy gown.

Heat claimed her. "Why?"

"Because I want to spend some time taking this hot dress off you, and it'll probably take most of the night."

"Then let's go to my place."

He kissed her. "Your place have popcorn?"

"Yes, my sky pilot, it does."

He drove them away from the restaurant. She waved at her father and Mr. Zola standing by the door, then cuddled close to her soon-to-be husband.

He said, "Forgot something."

"What?"

"Forgot to say, I love you, Counselor."

"I love you, too."

Soaring on the wings of happiness, Anita looked forward to their future.

* * * * *

Dear Reader,

Haven't we all fantasized about vacationing in some exotic location with a gorgeous companion? I know I have! Other than the fun fantasy part of the story, I hope you will see the evolution of a butterfly that has been stuck in her cocoon for far too long. I thoroughly enjoyed developing Connie into Contessa and revealing the multifaceted person just below the surface of her staid persona.

I guess, in some ways, their relationship is a reflection of my personal belief that you must always trust your inner voice. Just as Michael had to learn to ignore his eyes and listen to his heart.

I hope you will enjoy reading *Fiji Fantasy* and getting to know Michael and (Contessa) Connie. Feel free to let me know what you think by emailing me at eoverton03@yahoo.com. I look forward to your comments.

Elaine Overton

FIJI FANTASY

Elaine Overton

Chapter 1

*E*eegh! *Eeegh! Eeegh!*

Connie Vaughn reached across the nightstand and hit the snooze button on her alarm clock, as her eyes popped open. She was wide-awake, and anyone who knew her well understood this was a rare occurrence. Most mornings, her alarm clock got knocked across the room before Connie even considered actually getting out of bed. She was not a morning person.

But today was different. Today was the day. The one she'd been patiently waiting on and planning for years. Later, she would board a plane alone heading to the tiny island of Fiji where she would spend the next seven days celebrating her thirtieth birthday.

A small tap on her door brought up her head off the pillow. "Come in."

Annie, her sister-in-law of three years, peeked her head around the door. "Morning, I was frying some eggs and wondered if you wanted any?"

Connie smiled at her unexpected ally. Looking back, Connie was pretty sure this trip never would've happened without Annie's unwavering support.

"No, thanks." Connie sat up in the bed, bracing herself on her elbows. "I want to get to work early. I have a lot to do before I leave."

At the reminder that today was the day, Annie's eyes twinkled and took on a faraway look and Connie knew her sister-in-law was contemplating a full week alone with her husband. Something the poor woman hadn't experienced since moving into Brian's house three years ago.

After Annie left, Connie hopped out of bed with high energy. She was feeling an excitement that was increasingly hard to contain. She crossed the room and locked her bedroom door before reaching under the bed and pulling out her suitcase. She propped it on the bed and opened it, breathing a sigh of pleasure at the array of colorful outfits she'd bought just for the occasion. The contents of the medium-size brown suitcase had cost a small fortune, but to Connie it was money well spent.

Looking down at the neatly packed bag, she knew that this week would be the one and only time she would ever wear these clothes. Never again would she have the nerve to wear expensive designer clothes.

Considering her forty-thousand-dollar-a-year salary as a personal assistant, Connie knew that spending that kind of money on clothes was ridiculously extravagant. And yet she did not regret a single penny of it.

She picked up the small matching scraps of clothing sitting on top of the others and unfolded them into a tiny two-piece, hot-pink bikini. She smiled to herself, realizing the little thing would barely covered her most private parts. Her brother, Brian, her aunt Rita and even Annie would all be scandalized to know that she had bought the bathing suit precisely because it revealed so much.

She glanced at the clock and saw that it was six forty-seven; she wanted to be at work by seven-thirty. She neatly repacked the bikini and stood staring down at it for several seconds before deciding, Why not?

Quickly she slipped her flannel gown over her head, pulled off her cotton underwear and put on the bikini. Tying the halter top behind her neck, she walked across the room to the full-length mirror that covered the back of her closet door and her small smile widened to a grin.

She'd bought the bathing suit one year ago, and every night since then, she'd been putting herself through a rigorous exercise routine, sit-ups, leg lifts and twenty minutes on the treadmill that sat in the far corner of the room.

She had a naturally slender build, but the lack of activity in her life had left her soft and flabby. But, the woman she saw in the mirror now did not have an ounce of flab on her. Her petite body was as toned as a professional athlete. And although she'd been raised to believe vanity was a sin, at this particular moment, Connie chose to ignore that teaching. Because she looked good, and was feeling quite proud of it! She turned this way and that, looking at herself from every angle. Yep, damn good!

She covered her mouth to suppress a giggle that had bubbled up from nowhere. This trip would be the fulfillment of her every dream. For once in her life, she had a chance to be happy. A one-week extravaganza, but that was okay, because she would make the most of this time. Even if it were only for a few days, it would have to be enough. She would make it enough.

This was her single chance to be…free.

A short time later, Connie entered the kitchen, dressed in a black, polyester pantsuit with a light gray shell underneath the jacket that matched her loafers. Her shoulder-length hair was twisted in a tight bun at the back of her head, and the only jewelry she wore was a small cross around her neck unless you counted her glasses.

"Good morning." She came up behind her brother and placed a light kiss on his cheek.

"Good morning, Connie," Brian Vaughn muttered. Folding the morning paper he was reading, he laid it beside his plate on the table and took in his sister's appearance with one glance. "You look nice today."

"Thank you." She gave her automated response to her brother's daily comment. Connie knew she did not look nice, she looked like exactly what she was. An exceptionally efficient personal assistant. But every morning Brian commented that she looked nice, for lack of anything better to say. She appreciated the effort.

Annie turned from the stove holding a sizzling skillet in her hand. "Sure you don't want any breakfast?" she asked again, as she slid the fried eggs onto her husband's plate.

"No, thanks." She glanced at the clock on the wall above the stove. "I've got to get going. I just wanted to say goodbye…this is the last time I will see you for a week." Her eyes quickly slid to her brother and then away.

"I still don't like this." Brian frowned while using the side of his fork to cut into his fried eggs. "Why would a single woman want to travel so far by herself with what's going on in the world? Every time I turn on the news, I hear a story of a woman being accosted in some strange land."

Connie pursed her lips, but otherwise held her peace. Brian had been trying to talk her out of this trip from the moment she had announced it. And she should've expected him to try again this morning. Brian wouldn't be Brian if he didn't try one final time.

"I'll be fine." She reached over and covered his hand resting beside his plate.

"I just don't like the idea of you going away by yourself."

"I'm single, Brian. If I don't go anywhere by myself, then I'll never go anywhere."

He arched an eyebrow. "And is that such a bad thing? You don't see me and Annie traipsing all over the earth looking for trouble."

"That's because we can't afford to," Annie said laughingly, even as she turned off the stove and picked up her own plate to join them at the table. "Connie has been saving for this for years, Brian. Probably dreaming about it for longer than that." Annie caught her husband's eye across the table and shook her head. "Let's not spoil it for her."

Once again, Connie was grateful for whatever twist of fate had brought her sister-in-law into her life. Unlike Brian who was her own flesh and blood, Annie knew that this was more than a vacation. It was a time for an untested dove to try her wings.

For the first time in her life, she was doing something totally out of character of ultracompetent Connie. For once, she was doing something just for herself and she was not about to let Brian talk her out of it this time.

She was thirty years old and had never been outside the state of Connecticut. She'd worked in the same job with the same company since finishing business school at the age of twenty. She'd lived with her brother almost her entire life, from the time their parents died when Connie was twelve until now, barring that brief six-month nightmare in which she found herself married to and living with a sociopath posing as a perfectly sane accountant.

She'd met Nathan Moore when he had joined their church less than six years ago. He was average looking, and at first he had seemed a really nice man. But nothing probably would've come of their acquaintance if Brian hadn't taken to bringing him home to dinner a couple times a week. It didn't take Connie long to realize her brother was playing matchmaker and, although there was nothing particularly interesting or appealing about Nathan, in a strange way, Connie thought his very blandness was a good sign. In her ignorance of men, she had missed many of the signs that he was trouble. Signs a more experienced woman may have picked up on right away.

Like his subtle suggestions about what she wore. The small criticisms he offered as advice. His volatile temper that she first dismissed as the stresses of his job as a Certified Public Accountant for the city of Hartford. At least, that was always the explanation he would offer in those more-sane moments and, needing some sense of understanding, Connie was eager to grab on to any excuse.

And after just over eight months of dating, they married in a small ceremony at their church. Brian was his best man.

It wasn't long after the wedding that Nathan's premarital suggestions became commands. And the mood swings became more extreme and occurred more often, and eventually he just stopped offering any explanation. And the criticisms became abusive.

And Connie learned one of the hardest lessons of her life. That of all the different types of abuse, emotional abuse was the hardest to prove. After all, it was mostly done with words, and in the privacy of their home. But the effect it had on her already fragile self-esteem was devastating. She became depressed, and stopped caring about her appearance. After all, nothing she ever did pleased him anyway.

Of course, Nathan used her lack of interest in…*anything* against her. Convincing Brian, and everyone else they knew, that this was why they were getting divorced after only six months of marriage. *Connie just wasn't willing to put forth the effort to make their marriage work.*

Connie didn't have the energy or desire to fight him. She just packed up her most precious possessions and moved back in with her brother. Less than a year later, Brian met and married Annie and the three of them settled into a small family unit. And although she'd toyed with the idea of moving out, maybe even leaving the state of Connecticut, she never did. She just dreamed and hoped that, one day, life would present her with the opportunity for something…exciting.

It finally came two months ago when she won the daily lottery for ten thousand dollars, playing the same number she'd played for almost five years. Her wedding date. And the irony, that finally her marriage to Nathan was paying off, was not lost on her.

Of course, Brian had expected her to just put that money in the bank to gain interest and be a safety net. But then, Brian didn't know—nor would he have approved, if he had—that this was the opportunity she'd been waiting for.

This was her time to shine, her time for a little island fantasy. And she had every intention of living it to the fullest. For one glorious week, she was going to lock staid assistant Connie in the closet and bring out hedonist Contessa. She was going to eat as much as she wanted, drink as much as she wanted, do anything she wanted to and that included having sex for the first time in five years! And…as much as she wanted to.

Chapter 2

Contessa was almost certain there was a silly grin on her face, but she found it impossible to wipe it off. Everything about her trip so far had surpassed her expectations. Her first-class flight to the big island of Viti Levu had been relaxing. The limousine ride to the harbor was comfortable, and now she was on a luxury ship being ferried to the resort island itself, while sipping on an iced tea. *Life was sweet.*

Her eyes lit up as the resort began to come into view. It was even more beautiful than the pictures in the brochure. At first glance, the hotel looked like something out of a science-fiction novel, all shiny steel and glass. It towered over the palm trees and lush green foliage that seemed to be everywhere. In the distance, she could see a line of mountains that were the essence of rugged beauty, reaching for the sky.

As they drew closer, she could see the bay and convinced herself that she could even make out the pods below the surface. When she had first read about the construction of an underwater hotel in Fiji, it had been years ago and she thought the idea was fascinating in a vague way. After all, it was not like she would ever be in any position to afford to stay there.

And yet…here she was!

A short while later, she was in the elevators being lowered to her underwater suite. She stared out through the window at the fish swimming by in total disregard of the intruders that had taken over their home. The fish were so close, and the water so clear, she felt she could almost reach out and touch them. And she wondered, How this was possible? What type of brilliant engineer could've designed such a structure?

Absently, she felt the glass wall of the elevator just as the doors behind her opened and she found herself standing in a hotel lobby. Intellectually, she understood that yes, it was a hotel and therefore it would have a lobby. But her eyes told a different story.

If she turned her head right, she was staring out into the Poseidon Bay; if she turned her head left, she was in a hotel. She chuckled to herself at the sheer wonder of it all and, although her unexpected outburst had drawn the eyes of other passengers to her, she didn't care. Connie knew that if she had to go right back up in the elevator and leave the island today, she would still consider it a trip well made.

Several hours later, she stood in front of the full-length mirror in her suite staring at the woman looking back at her. It had to be the island, she decided. She looked different. She felt different. She *was* different.

It was almost as if, with every mile they flew farther from Connecticut, she was transforming into the beautiful, confident woman who stood before her. Free.

There was that word again, she thought. Whenever she tried to find the word to describe how she felt it was *free*. Did that mean when she was at home, she was shackled in some way?

She shook off the morbid thought, and focused on the image before her. Connie had always known what colors and clothes best accented her features, despite the fact that she typically never used the knowledge. But now, looking at the end result…she was stunned by how unfamiliar she felt to herself. Unfamiliar but great.

She picked up her small clutch purse and headed to the door. The hotel concierge had given her the name of a popular nightclub and now she was heading there. So far, she had not had a single regret regarding her trip. She could only hope that by morning she still felt the same.

He noticed her the moment she entered the club. It was hard not to. Michael imagined the scene before him must've been something like watching Cleopatra enter her temple. Every eye in the place turned and followed her descent down the spiral stairs and across the crowded room.

Dressed in a little midthigh black sequin number that clung to her hourglass figure as if painted on, her auburn tresses were pinned up at the back of her head in some type of complicated arrangement, but all Michael could think about was how it would look hanging down around her shoulders. With her hair up, it revealed the halter top of her dress tied in a perfect bow behind her neck and brought to mind exactly what she looked like. A gift dropped from heaven. Her elegantly shaped legs were encased in fishnet stockings and shiny black stilettos. She wore a thin gold chain with some type of charm dangling from it, stud diamond earrings and carried a small black bag. The rest was all flawless copper-gold skin. She was stylish yet understated. A combination Michael had seen few women manage to pull off. She wasn't a tall or imposing woman, yet there was something quite striking in her appearance.

She was beautiful, but it wasn't just her physical beauty that caught his attention, it was her confidence. It wasn't vanity…exactly. Just assurance of her worth.

The lights flashed, the music blared, bodies bounced

around her and yet she walked with all the urgency of some-one taking a morning stroll through a park. She had her pick of the men and knew it. Her eyes darted from one hopeful soul to another, often accompanied by a soft come-hither smile. She was deciding, debating, and Michael rose from his seat, fully intending to enter the competition before she made up her mind.

He'd been on the island for two days, and during that time his mind had been completely occupied with his new job. The lovely lady coming toward him had done what seemed impossible. She'd taken his mind off his troubles, and he wasn't about to watch her walk out of the club on the arm of another man.

Quickly he worked his way through the crowd at a forty-five-degree angle to her, intending to cut her off. Being one of the tallest men in the room had its advantages as he was able to keep her in his sights the entire time.

She stopped and so did Michael, feeling his heart quicken as she turned and looked up into the hungry eyes of the man swaying gently next to her. He had the appearance of a local, with his Polynesian good looks, and long dark hair. Michael felt his eyes narrowing, and fought down some primal desire to pounce on the man for daring to look at his Cleopatra with such blatant sexual desire. Managing to suppress the unex-pected emotion, he continued to move across the floor until he was standing at her other side.

The couple beside him was still locked in some kind of unspoken connection. The local was patiently waiting for the beautiful woman to give him some sign of acceptance, she was still deciding.

Michael touched her hand and, as expected, her eyes turned toward him. They were light, even in the dark club he could see a translucent quality to them. A dark eyebrow arched in si-lent offense of his forwardness and Michael couldn't help but smile. His Cleopatra comparison seemed more apt than ever.

"Good evening."

The other eyebrow went up. "Do I know you?"

His smile turned to a grin. "Would you like to?" He glanced at the local, who was now giving him a hard glare.

He couldn't care less, the beauty's attention was now on him and he planned to keep it that way. She took him in with one thorough glance and since she didn't immediately turn back to the local, Michael assumed he'd passed inspection.

He leaned forward slightly, just close enough to whisper in her ear. "I'm Michael, by the way."

She glanced back at the local and then to Michael again before answering. "Contessa."

Michael felt like a weight had been lifted off his chest as he watched the local turn toward another woman dancing beside him. Apparently, the man realized—just as Michael had—that she'd made her choice.

He knew he was taking a chance, but some instinct guided him to lift her hand to his lips and place a soft kiss on her knuckles. "Nice to meet you, Contessa. Can I buy you a drink?"

To his surprise, she pulled her hand from his, but instead of stepping back, she stepped forward and placed both arms around his neck. "I'd rather dance."

Michael couldn't seem to stop smiling. "Your wish is my command."

He turned slightly, pulling her close against his body and was pleased to realize one of his favorite songs was playing, Cee Lo's "Bright Lights Bigger City."

As her soft, warm body moved against his, Michael was amazed by how right she felt in his arms. The top of her head was right beneath his chin in her spiky heels. It was as if she was made to be held by him and it took every ounce of his strength not to move in closer to her body, to feel more of her pressed against him, to give in to all the recurring primal urges this woman seemed to bring out in him.

He felt her arms tightened around his neck, but he tried to maintain the little distance between them, afraid that if she realized how quickly his body was reacting to her closeness, it would scare her off.

He inhaled deeply trying to identify her fragrance, but it eluded him. It was faintly familiar, but he had a feeling her own natural scent was mixing with the perfume to create the uniquely intoxicating blend.

Her slender arms tightened around his neck as her body moved against his. Her shapely hips gyrated back and forth and as if hypnotized by the erotic motion, his large hands floated down until they held her between them.

He glanced back at her face to realize her eyes were closed and she was apparently lost in the music. Somehow in the past few minutes, as she so sensually savored the music, she had become even more beautiful than the woman that had first entered the club.

It was taking every bit of decency Michael possessed to resist what was seemingly offered. But somehow he managed to hold the distance between them. The lyrics seeped into his mind and nudged him forward.

He swallowed hard, as his large hands gently squeezed the soft flesh between his palms. She was so soft and perfectly round in all the places a woman should be. His mind could not resist imaging what the copper skin would look like against his white sheets. Imaging her perfect body beneath his. Imaging her gyrating hips moving for a totally different reason.

They were surrounded by people and yet she was all that he was aware of. Her scent wafted around them, her soft body cradled against his. Contessa.

Michael knew she was unlike any woman he'd met in a long time. There was something so genuine and free-spirited about her. He knew where this evening was going to end, and so did she. There were no games being played, no deliberate teasing. She was a woman fully in control of her sexuality. She knew what she wanted and how to get it. She'd come here tonight looking for a bed partner and fully intended to leave with one. Michael had every intention of being that man.

Throwing up her arms in the air, she twisted out of his reach, so caught up in the music he was not even sure she was aware that almost every man in the place had stopped to watch her dance. Michael couldn't do anything about them watching. Hell, he couldn't fault them, either. But he already knew if any of them made a move on her, someone was going to get hurt.

Just as the song ended, she spun back around to him and her beautiful face spread in a wide smile. A thin sheen of sweat covered her body, making her look even more radiant. Michael knew he had to have her.

He took her hand again and asked, "How about that drink?" Fighting down his secret fear that he was only the first of many dances that night.

Her head tilted to the side as she seemed to consider it. It was the longest ten seconds of his life, but finally she smiled and nodded. "I guess I'm a little thirsty."

He stepped to the side allowing her to lead the way to the bar, and tried very hard to get his mind on drinks and off the oh-so-slowly-swaying backside in front of him. The woman was wrecking havoc on the iron-clad control he had until now taken great pride in.

He settled on a bar stool beside her.

"What are you having?" The bartender, a burly guy who—Michael knew from watching him throughout the night—despite his size, had the hands of a surgeon.

"Sex on the Beach?" he asked Contessa.

She shook her head. "I'm allergic to cranberries. Just a Manhattan."

"Two Manhattans."

As the bartender walked away, he turned on his stool. "So, Contessa, where are you from?"

She smiled knowingly. "Here and there. And you?"

"Connecticut."

Michael thought he saw her eyes widen slightly in surprise, but then it was gone before he could decide if it were real or imagined.

She leaned toward him and, in the lights of the bar, he could finally see the true color of her almond-shaped eyes— hazel-gold. They focused intently on his face, and Michael was stunned to realize she was even more lovely up close.

"Do you believe in fate, Michael?"

He almost smiled, believing she was joking, but something about the seriousness of her expression held him back. "I'm not sure."

"I do," she whispered, and the brief smile of a private joke flashed across her face before she sat back on her stool. "We all have a part to play in this strange thing called life. We all have our roles."

Michael's eyes widened, wondering if maybe this was not the first bar she'd been in that night. She was starting to sound as if she'd already had a couple drinks.

Just then the bartender set the Manhattans on the counter in front of them.

"I hate these things." Michael fished out the maraschino cherry and placed it on the napkin beside his drink, then took a sip. "So, what is your role?"

She smiled again and Michael realized he really could get addicted to those smiles. "Actually, I was wondering the same thing about you." She took a sip of her drink and very deliberately set it down, before reaching over to place her small hand on his thigh. "Are you a dream fulfiller, Michael?"

He caught himself just before his eyes drifted down to her cleavage, which was swelling over the top of her dress ever so nicely. "Depends on the dream?"

"Well…" Her hand slowly inched up his thigh, and Michael steeled himself against the urge to pick her up, sling her over his shoulder and carry her out of the place. What was it about this woman that gave him such crazy thoughts?

"I had this dream of having one wildly passionate night with a stranger."

Whoa. There it was. No game playing with this one. He took another sip of his drink and wondered if maybe he was the one dreaming. He looked up until his eyes met hers. "I think I can fulfill that dream, Contessa." He smiled.

She frowned. "You think?"

His smile faded slightly. What the hell did she want, a written guarantee? "I know I can."

She tilted her head to the side and studied him, then smiled that beautiful smile of hers. "I think you can, too." Still, he watched as her attention returned to the dance floor.

Hell, no. Michael instantly stood from his stool and stepped forward until he was standing next to her stool. Using his index finger, he lifted her chin until she was once again completely focused on him. Slowly, so as not to startle her, he lowered his lips until they touched hers.

It was a gentle kiss at first but, once he had a taste of her, he deepened it, needing to taste more. He could taste the drink on her lips but also her own unique flavor. Her soft, warm lips yielded beneath his, beckoning him in.

Her lips parted and his tongue slid inside her mouth like a hot knife through butter. At some point, he'd wrapped his arms around her small waist and pulled her up off her stool against his body. And now, the feel of her lining up against him shoulder to hip, combined with the intoxicating flavor of her kiss, was making him want more than he could possibly have in their current location.

She wasn't making matters any better, running her small hands through his curly hair the way she was. She wanted him as much as he wanted her.

"Come on, let's get out of here." Quickly taking some bills from his wallet, he threw them on the counter before taking her hand. He started pushing his way through the crowded dance floor but, during their time at the bar, more people had swarmed in and the club was twice as crowded as it had been just an hour before.

Michael just burrowed his way through them, opening a path for Contessa to follow. He was determined not to lose this beautiful angel in the crush of bodies surrounding them.

He tightly grasped her small hand, feeling the warmth of her skin against his. That primitive urging surfaced again, telling him to make sure he held on to her, and never let go.

Chapter 3

The night air against her heated skin was like a splash of water in the face. Connie took a deep breath and wondered what the hell was she doing? This man was a total stranger, she knew nothing about him and yet every instinct in her was comforted by his strong presence. Just as she'd allowed him to lead her out of the club with no resistance, somehow, she knew this was the man she'd come to Fiji looking for.

Lord knew he met her physical requirements. The man was gorgeous on steroids! If she'd been allowed to create a dream lover, she wasn't sure she could've come up with anything this good.

He was perfect, everything from the chiseled features of his dark face to his impressive build. His eyes were dark brown, deep brown, but still...kind.

His lips were slightly pouted, but not full to the point of looking feminine. There was nothing feminine about this man. Her eyes took in his lean, hard body once again. Nope, nothing at all.

And then there was his smell. Of all the things Connie thought attracted her to a man, she would've listed smell on the bottom of that list. But his smell was wonderful. Clean, masculine and yet so erotic it excited her as nothing else had.

She knew he thought it was the touch of his skin on hers that made her turn his way, when in fact it was his scent. The moment he came into her range, she had became some kind of animal sniffing the air for the scent of its mate. It was a bit embarrassing when she thought about it, but truly it was his wonderful smell that made her so forward, so fast.

She'd plan to take it slow, to spend the evening meeting various men and then make her decision tomorrow, but instead here she was following a man she'd met less than thirty minutes ago back to…

"Damn." Suddenly he stopped, and Connie just avoided colliding into his broad back. He turned toward her and taking her face between his hands, lowered his lips to hers. Connie clutched his silk shirt, feeling his hard abs beneath her fingers and focused on the erotic sensations floating through her body. The man kissed like an angel.

He was all warm heat and sweetness. His touch, his taste, his smell were all combining into some kind of addictive formula that she suddenly could not get enough of.

She felt his large hands sliding over her body, touching, stroking and all she wanted to do was turn into his hands, so he could touch more of her. She was suddenly craving him with an intensity that left her breathless. His mouth left hers, but she gasped when she felt his hot breath on her neck, her chin, behind her ear. She shivered with a desire that had apparently been so repressed and suppressed she had not realized it even existed.

The last tiny bit of sanity she had seemed to flee her as she tugged at his shirt, pulling it from his slacks, needing to feel his skin against hers.

Thankfully, he seemed to still be thinking. Because he

gently pushed her back, and taking her hand once again dragged her along behind him.

She frowned slightly as they reached the parking lot, but continued on. "Where are we going?"

"My yacht is docked off the pier over there." He gestured farther down where several boats were lined.

"Your yacht?"

He stopped suddenly again and, turning to her, lifted her up in his arms. It happened so suddenly, Connie had to clutch his shoulders to regain her equilibrium.

"I just can't seem to stop kissing you," he said, continuing to move forward even as his lips came down on hers.

Without hesitation, Connie wrapped her arms around his neck and pulled his head down to hers, taking his tongue into her mouth. She moaned low in her throat, savoring the taste of him. His mouth moved over hers, before his teeth nipped at her bottom lip. And his large hand gently stroked her hip.

The sound of a horn beeping startled both of them, and Connie realized that during their heated exchanged they'd managed to walk right into the parking-lot traffic.

Michael spun around with lightning speed, swinging her up and out of harm's way, and she clutched at his shoulders even more. Once he was between the safety of two parked cars, he stopped and leaned back against one. Connie could feel his heart beating rapidly against her breast.

He laughed, placing his forehead against hers. "You make me crazy, you know that?"

"You do the same thing to me." She placed a hand against his cheek, looking into his eyes. They were so expressive, his lust, his humor, it was all reflected right there.

He lowered her to her feet once again. "If we want to get out of this parking lot safely, then I think I better not touch you."

She smiled, feeling more feminine and desirable than she had in more years than she could remember. She sauntered a few feet away, and turned to gesture with her finger for him to follow.

He did. No longer even trying to hide his wandering eyes. They covered every inch of her body and Connie felt like wherever his eyes landed, her skin heated beneath his hungry stare.

As they reached the pier, Connie slowed, realizing she did not know which boat was his. She turned back, and smiling knowingly, he pointed to a large white yacht at the end of the pier. It was the largest boat in the dock, but she kept that observation to herself, wondering what he did for a living.

She would not ask, no matter how curious she became. After all, this was supposed to be a no-strings-attached weekend, and knowing too much about the man would definitely be *stringy*.

She continued on down the dock until she came to his boat. Michael stepped into the boat first, before reaching back and gently lifting her over. Connie gripped his hard shoulders to balance and, instead of releasing her, Michael just held her in his arms, body to body.

He looked deep into her eyes, and whispered, "Are you real?"

She smiled. "Do I feel real?"

His large hand wandered down her side, gliding over her hip and down her leg. "Well, you feel real." He leaned forward and kissed her, but this kiss was different, more forceful, demanding that she open her mouth to his and she did. After a moment, he lifted his head and sighed. "You taste real." He shook his head in mock consternation. "But, still, I just don't know. You're too beautiful to be real."

Connie felt her eyes softening. The little things like being complimented by a man who desired her. How had she managed to live without these things for so long? She wondered if maybe that was why she had reacted so quickly to Michael.

Was it just that she was more hungry for affection than she had realized?

He lowered her to her feet, and the sensual look in his eyes left no doubt in her mind what he wanted, and she had every intention of giving it to him. "I guess there is one way to find out."

Connie glanced around the ultraclean interior of the yacht. There seemed to be cream-colored leather, chrome and cherrywood everywhere. And it was all shined to military perfection.

"This is really nice." She glanced through one of the windows to the lower deck.

"Thanks." He went to the stairs leading there and took the first step down. She started to follow, but then he turned to her, and she realized the playful flirt of a moment ago had disappeared. His face was solemn and serious. Cupping her face in his chin, he looked directly into her eyes.

"Do you really want to do this, Contessa?"

She smiled softly, realizing she'd made the right choice. This was not a man who would force himself on a woman. He was giving her a chance to leave if she wanted. Little did he know, that was the furthest thought from her mind.

"I want you, Michael." She took a deep breath and decided to confess. "More than I've ever wanted any man. So, yes, I definitely want to do this."

He turned and continued down the stairs. Connie bit her lip to hold back an excited smile and followed him. The lower level was even more impressive that the upper deck. More leather, chrome and cherrywood, but there were also a few of the comforts of home. The captain's bed which was built into the wall was covered in white linens including a fully white duvet turned back ever-so-welcomingly.

Connie turned in a circle, as she glanced around the cabin once again. "Okay, who am I not seeing?"

"What? Are you saying I couldn't do this myself?"

She just gave him a knowing look.

Michael laughed. "I have a deckhand named George."

"Aah, and where is George tonight?"

"Not sure. He'll be back by morning. Why do you ask?"

"Just wondering." She turned to find Michael's eyes steadily trained on her. "So, we're alone."

He nodded, and stepped forward only until a slither of space existed between their bodies. "Completely."

He placed his large hands on her shoulders, and slowly lowered them down her bare arms, all the while his eyes were trained on hers. "I kinda rushed you out of the bar. Would you like a drink?"

She shook her head and smiled.

He smiled back. "Something to eat?"

She shook her head and smiled again.

"Hmm." He rubbed his chin thoughtfully. "Wanna watch some TV? Maybe a movie?"

She couldn't hold back a soft laugh. "Sure, why not."

His eyes widened in horror and surprise. "Really?"

She laughed openly and moved back until her knees came up against the edge of the bed. She shook her head. "That'll teach you to tease." And she fell on the bed.

Michael came to stand over her. "Lesson learned." He began unbuttoning his shirt. "You never did tell me where you were from."

He was trying to keep a running conversation, so the all-consuming hunger he knew must be reflected in his eyes did not alarm her.

"Yes, I did." She lifted her well-toned legs and kicked off one shoe with the other foot, and then repeated. Followed by removing her fishnets.

Watching her slender legs rise, Michael subconsciously licked his lips, getting just a sneak peek of the darkened area between her legs. He couldn't really see anything, but that didn't matter. He was getting hard just thinking about her soft femininity. Did she wax? Was she moist in anticipation of what was to come? He was about ready to burst out of his pants, so he truly hoped she was as hot for him as he was for her.

Just as she started to lower them, he took her legs and planted them firmly against his chest, letting his warm hands run over her calves. Her skin was like fine silk against his fingers. He swallowed hard, trying with every effort of will not to simply spread her legs and pounce on her.

Smart men did not pounce on Cleopatra, he thought. No, a smart man would savor her abundant riches, and Michael had every intention of savoring the hell out of her.

He pulled off his shirt and tossed it carelessly on the floor. "No, you did not." He shook his head, returning to their previous conversation.

"I said here and there." She smiled mischievously. The sexy little thing knew he was fishing for information about her. Who could blame him?

"What's the weather like in here and there?" he asked the question playfully, but he really was wanting to know more about her.

She laughed again, that light musical laugh that only inflamed his already inflamed senses. One of her legs slowly slid up his chest.

"It's hot," she whispered seductively and Michael felt his cock twitch beneath his slacks. He was somewhat startled to realize this woman could cause him to come with her voice alone.

It was a bit humbling, because as hard a time as he was having holding on to his self-control, he had the feeling she could take him or leave him. Even now.

Time to take control of the situation, he thought. He pulled her legs around his waist and leaned over her. He had the added pleasure of looking directly into her lust-filled hazel eyes. He touched his lips to her.

Michael felt more than saw her intense response to it. Her whole body reacted to the kiss. Her back arched, her arms wrapped around his neck and Michael carefully lowered his full weight onto her. She was in no way his first woman, but feeling her soft breasts against his bare chest, feeling her legs slide along his pants legs, he was feeling fifteen again.

His open mouth found hers, his tongue teased her top lip until she parted her lips under his and he plunged into her mouth tasting her unique flavor. She moaned softly, and Michael could hold back no longer.

His mouth roamed over her neck, outlining her cheek-bone with his tongue, even as his eager fingers toyed with the pretty bow at the back of her neck. It took some concentrated skill, but he finally felt the knot come undone and sat up on his side to look down into her dazed face.

He smiled, and she smiled back. He wanted to take it slow, he wanted to make this last, knowing on some instinctual level that Contessa was something unique. Something he would not experience again for a long time, if ever, after to-night.

Without taking his eyes from hers, he slowly lowered the halter top of her dress, folding it back away from her body before finally allowing his eyes to lower to her breasts. Like everything else about her, her breasts were perfect. Her light brown nipples were hardened and standing straight up begging for his mouth to taste. And he did. First one, then the other, squeezing the soft flesh with his hands. She twisted beneath him, tangling her fingers in his short curls, holding him to her as she panted with desire.

Michael rolled away from her and sat up long enough to divest himself of the rest of his clothing. As he pulled a condom from the drawer of his nightstand, Michael could feel her eyes on him even though she did not say a word. When he'd donned the condom and rolled back over to look at her, her eyes stayed on him. Silently examining that part of him that most wanted her attention, before she reached over and gripped him in her small hand. Wrapping her fingers around him, Michael was frozen in place, struggling to breathe.

She was still wearing her dress, although now it only covered half her body. Michael slid his hand beneath the bottom, sliding it up her leg and she parted her thighs invitingly. The fabric moved with his arm slowly rising. He smiled suddenly and looked up into her eyes.

"Hot pink." He ran his hand over the front of her panties. "Nice."

She returned the smile. "It's my favorite color."

Swallowing hard, he slid his hand beneath the silky fabric seeking her heat, her fire. And he found it quickly soaked in anticipation. Michael knew if he did not move fast, it would be too late. He removed the pink fabric, tossing it aside, and slid into her.

Her back arched again, as her legs wrapped around his thighs. Her arms wrapped around his neck and two bodies became one. Bracing his weight on his arms, Michael pushed deeper, wondering what Heaven could possibly offer to rival this.

She was so responsive, so welcoming and as hungry for him as he was for her. The farther he pushed into her body, the more she opened herself up to accommodate him. They quickly settled into a rhythm, each giving as good as they took.

Feeling the orgasm coming quickly, far too quickly, Michael buried his head against her throat as he let himself be carried away to paradise.

Chapter 4

She was awakened by the sound of the waves crashing against the side of the yacht. At first, Connie did not know where she was and then suddenly it all came rushing to the forefront of her brain. Slowly, she opened her eyes and found dark brown eyes staring back.

He smiled, and it lit his handsome face. "Morning, beautiful."

Connie smiled in return. "Is it morning?"

He nodded slowly.

Wow. It seemed like it had only been a few minutes, when in fact it had been several hours. Apparently, she'd slept like the dead. She stretched leisurely, feeling better than she had in years. Some part of her knew her reaction was completely wrong. After all, she was thousands of miles from home, waking up in the bed of a stranger. It was so different from her typical behavior, even she didn't recognize herself. And yet it felt amazingly right. She chuckled to herself, imaging Brian's reaction.

"What?" he asked, sitting up and bracing himself on one elbow.

She looked at him and smiled again. The man really was everything she'd hoped for and more. She shrugged off the question and sat, taking the sheet with her.

"Hungry?"

She laughed remembering the conversation of the night before. "What's with you and food?"

He laughed. "I don't know, it just seems like I should say something." His eyes fanned over her body. "You probably won't believe this but I don't do this all the time."

She leaned forward and placed a quick kiss on his lips. "You're right. I don't believe it." She scooted to the edge of the bed, taking the duvet with her. "I better get going."

A sheet still covered his midsection, but it did nothing to conceal his renewed interest in her. "What's the hurry? I was hoping we could spend some time together today."

Now standing, Connie glanced back at him looking like something straight out of her fantasies. He was perfectly, almost exactly, what she'd wanted. She could not have asked for a more attractive man, or a more attentive lover. But the problem was that some self-preservation instinct in her told her that Michael was more than just a pretty face. More than just a one-night-stand kinda guy. From what she'd seen so far, in addition to his looks, he was charming and intelligent. In short, he was the kind of man that left a trail of broken hearts scattered wherever he went. And the last thing Connie wanted was to get emotionally involved with a man—even a man as exceptional as this one seemed to be. It could only end in disaster.

No, it was better to take her wonderful memories of the night before and move on to the next Michael. "Actually, I had plans for the day—but thanks anyway." She scuttled across the floor headed to the bathroom, making an awkward display of trying to pick up her clothing as well as maintain a hold on the duvet as she went.

Michael watched as she gently closed the bathroom door and finally he stood naked from the bed. Even flustered and embarrassed she was a gorgeous woman. And she made love like the world was ending tomorrow. He definitely wanted to see more of her, but just now as she'd blown him off, he'd had the distinct impression she was dismissing him—for good.

But why? He considered himself a pretty fair judge of people, and everything said she'd enjoyed last night as much as he did. Maybe she really did have plans for the day. He would try again when she reappeared. Otherwise, he would just have to take the dismissal for what it was.

He quickly picked out something to wear while he was waiting for her to come out of the bathroom. He selected a pair of dark brown shorts and a brown and orange Hawaiian shirt, laying them on the bed. It was going to be another perfect day in paradise, and he was going scuba diving later in the day.

He pulled his cell phone out of his pants pocket and checked his messages. The first one was from Tony.

"Hey, man, not going to make it this weekend. Long story, but I'll tell you about it when you get back. Sorry to drop you like this, check you later."

Michael shook his head. This was not the first time Tony had canceled on him. And Michael had a sneaky suspicion the long story would involve Tony's ex-girlfriend, Kena. She had a nasty habit of trying to control Tony's life.

He glanced at the bathroom door. Well, at least Tony's cancellation would free up more time to spend with beautiful Contessa. He realized she never did answer his question about being hungry. Maybe they could have breakfast and then spend the day together.

He walked over and, as he got closer, he could hear the

shower water running. He knocked softly but not one answered. He opened the door slightly. "Hello?"

He peeked his head around the corner of the door, really
just intending to ask her about breakfast, but seeing her soapy
silhouette through the glass doors caused him to completely
lose his train of thought.

She glanced over and noticed him naked in the doorway.
As provocative as a siren, she gave him an inviting half smile
and then turned fully away from him, and using both arms
lifted her hair off her neck. And as expected, every ounce
of testosterone flowing in his veins responded to the purely
feminine behavior.

His feet moved forward of their own accord and, before he
realized his intent, he was opening the shower door. She gave
him another of those backward glances and moved closer to
the showerhead so that the water was flowing uninterrupted
over her body, rinsing away the soap.

When he just stood mesmerized by the sight, she looked
at him over her shoulder once more. "Coming in?"

Michael stepped into the shower and pulled her back
against his body until his throbbing erection was pressed
against her bottom. His arms reached under hers and around
to find two handfuls of firm breasts complete with hardened
nipples. He licked along her collarbone tasting soap and water,
and feeling like he was about to explode if he did not get inside her at that moment.

She looked up at him, her soft lips slightly parted and inviting, and he accepted. Tasting her mouth gently at first and
then more forcefully as she responded in that wonderfully
open way she had about her. He could feel his heart beating
against his chest and realized that this woman excited him
more than anyone had in a long time. He guided her against
the wall, his hands roaming over every bit of her exceptional
body. Absently, he realized she must work out.

Using his arm, he lifted one leg and entered her body,

pushing her firmly against the wall, he drove into her repeatedly. Wanting the exquisite experience to last, he slowed his movements, but when she laid her head back against his shoulder, expressing her pleasure with a soft whimpering, Michael knew he would not be able to hold out much longer.

He pushed deeper inside her with each thrust until, just as he was about to come, he felt her whole body go rigid in his arms and realized she was there, too. Using every ounce of strength he possessed, he fought to hold them there together—one single perfect moment in two lives.

Contessa soon had her suspicions confirmed. In addition to being a fantastic lover, Michael was pretty fantastic at everything else. Against her better judgment, Contessa had allowed him to talk her into spending some time together. It was supposed to just be breakfast at a nearby restaurant that sat on a hill and overlooked a bluff. But as they were leaving the restaurant, they noticed some surfers off the shore and walked down to the beach to watch them for a while.

Connie was surprised to find that Michael had apparently toyed with surfing a little in his youth and he was able to explain some of the maneuvers of the surfers, things she would've never understood without someone insightful to explain them.

Connie thought that was where she should leave their morning, promising to meet him later that night for drinks. But when she mentioned she was taking her first scuba diving lesson that morning, Michael asked to come along.

An hour later she discovered that like everything else in his life apparently, Michael was also good at scuba diving. In a class of ten people and one instructor trying to coach everyone at once, Michael soon took over her instruction. Gently guiding her deeper and deeper. Behind her goggles her eyes widened at the colorful array of sea life in the turquoise waters.

Later that afternoon, they returned to his yacht and Connie met George, who turned out to be an older man who'd spent his whole life sailing in one form or another. Apparently George had known Michael since he was a young man growing up in Connecticut.

That was something that had disturbed Connie from the first. What were the chances that her island lover would be from Connecticut? It was a strange coincidence, and even as George regaled her with stories of a younger and much wilder Michael, she kept her questions to herself, fearing if she asked personal questions, Michael would feel free to do the same.

They took the yacht out of the harbor for a few hours, and as they sailed just off the coast of Malolo, Connie was once again struck by the beauty of the place. All these small islands, each unique and so scenic in their own way, it was surprising that they'd remained for the most part in their original form for so long.

George fixed a small Greek salad for lunch and the threesome ate and chatted about any number of topics, but Connie studiously avoided letting the conversation move toward the too personal. By the time they returned to the harbor, Connie knew she was in trouble.

The pink sunset in the distance was like something out of a picture frame, she was gliding through tropical waters aboard the yacht of a handsome man, who currently had eyes only for her. And somewhere in the deepest recesses of her mind, Connie understood she was already lost. By now she had fully intended to be on to her next conquest, but the problem was she didn't want to move on. She wanted to continue to spend the rest of the day with the fascinating, gorgeous man sitting across from her and *that* was a problem.

She'd known that morning—just looking at him—she had known that this was the kind of man women fell in love with. He probably had never met a woman he couldn't melt with his smile alone. This man was a highly skilled player, and a proficient heartbreaker—but he was not the future, at least not hers. And she had not spent an astronomical amount of money to travel halfway around the world just to go home lovesick. This trip was supposed to be about sowing her wild oats, not meeting the love of her life.

Connie recognized and understood all these things from an intellectual point of view, but Contessa…well, she was another story. Contessa recognized Prince Charming when she saw him. And right now, Prince Charming was sitting across the table from her laughing at something his cabin man had said. It was a rich baritone laugh, full of life and perfect, like every damn thing about the man. Yes, she thought with a heavy sigh, she was already lost.

Intentions aside, she ended up spending the evening with Michael. She returned to her hotel long enough to get dressed for an evening on the town. He picked her up a couple hours later and took her to the island of Suva where they spent the evening barhopping along the street named Victoria Parade. They did not stay longer than forty-five minutes in any one place, but the vibrant, festive atmosphere of people and night-clubs was intoxicating in itself.

After midnight, they walked down to Tiko's Floating Restaurant on the water and had a late dinner, consisting of the best crab legs Connie had ever tasted in her life. Then they sailed back to Paradise Island and Connie's underwater suite.

Hours later, Connie lay curled against Michael's body, cocooned in the warmth of his strong arms watching the fish float by her window. They'd made love twice that night and she could hear from his steady breathing that he had finally fallen asleep. But it was too late.

It was after he'd told her part of his life story. Despite her attempts to dissuade him, Michael had been determined to share some of who he was with her. He told her about his life in Hartford, and named so many places she knew well. But she never let him know that.

He told her about going off to Purdue University, and she found herself slightly envious of his college experience. He'd enjoyed all the pleasures of a good-looking, wealthy young man on his own for the first time, including the fraternity he had joined, members of which still comprised his inner circle of friends. He told her how he'd spent his life basically enjoying *life*. It was exactly the kind of life she'd imagined he'd had…charmed. With his words, he shared his experiences with her and by the time he began to make love to her for the second time, she knew she was in love.

The next morning, Connie was just getting out of the shower when she heard a knock on her door. She opened it to find a large bouquet of roses being held up.

"Where did you find those?" she asked in stunned surprise.

He laughed. "Where else? A florist." He followed her inside and placed the bouquet on a nearby table. "I was hoping to catch you before you went to breakfast."

He turned to face her and only then noticed that she was wearing a towel and nothing else. "Well, well, what have we here?" His dark eyes roamed over her body as if the towel did not exist. She smiled in return, wondering at how comfortable and at ease she felt with him.

He crossed the room to stand before her and lightly touched his finger to a spot of water on her shoulder. "Hmm… Seems I came a few minutes too late."

Her smile widened as she dropped the towel, letting it fall to the floor. "That look in your eyes is dirty enough, guess I'll have to wash again." She turned and darted back into the bathroom with Michael quickly pursuing.

An hour and a half later they were having breakfast in the hotel's underwater restaurant. The entire room was one big glass dome, and the sea life surrounding it swam over and around them. The turquoise water gave the room a neon glow. Although they were finished eating in less than an hour, they sat there for the next three hours, talking while diners came and left.

They spent the day exploring the island shops and sites hand in hand, and by that night, Connie had pretty much given up the fight to protect her heart and drenched herself in the novelty of pure, unadulterated happiness.

The next two days felt like a whirlwind as Michael pretty much moved himself from his yacht and into her underwater hotel suite and they never spent more than a few hours apart.

They took most of their meals in the hotel restaurant and spent hours talking about various aspects of their lives. It was during one of these discussions, that Connie accidentally mentioned that she was from Connecticut.

"Really?" Michael tilted his head to the side with a slight frown on his face. "Why didn't you mention it the other day? You know, when I told you that was where I was from?"

She poked at her garlic potatoes with her fork and shrugged. "I didn't know you that well."

His eyebrows rose slowly and he chuckled. "And you do now?"

"At least now I know enough about you to assume you're not a serial killer." She laughed and eventually the conversation moved on to new topics, but Connie was glad for the breakdown of that particular barrier because now she could tell him about her childhood. She'd never before considered how much her youth had influenced the woman she had become.

With Michael's competence in seemingly everything, Connie had found herself doing things she never would've tried alone. Snorkeling, paragliding, and he had even taught her how to drive his yacht, as they tooled around the smaller islands.

And the nights…the nights were incredible, as they held

each other and loved well into the morning hours. Often they would fall asleep in each other's arms and awaken in exactly the same position. As if they were both too afraid to move throughout the night, too afraid to break their fragile connection.

She knew it would eventually end, and when it did she would end up nursing the heartbreak of a lifetime. What she was feeling for Michael after only four days was stronger than anything she'd felt for Nathan during the entire time they'd been married. But even knowing that, she could not regret one moment of the time they spent together. Not one single moment.

Chapter 5

For the first time in his life, Michael realized he was in love, and with an incredible woman. Contessa was amazing. She was beautiful, intelligent, sophisticated and yet she still radiated a sweet wholesomeness that was equally attractive.

Not to mention her sense of taste and style was something straight off the runways of Paris. She always knew exactly what to wear for whatever occasion they had attended and she could affect any look from careless schoolgirl to regal princess. Whenever they went out, her unquestionable sense of style caused people—both men and women—to stop and stare, to compliment her appearance, to ask where she bought her clothes. Michael couldn't help the sense of pride he felt in her already, even though they were in no way committed to one another.

If someone had asked him to create a list of all the qualities he wanted in a woman, and then he'd compared that list to Contessa, he was certain he would mark off every category.

She was perfect and somehow by a strange twist of coincidence, she had landed right in his lap.

They had so much in common. They shared so many interests. Although Michael knew a lot of the things she was doing with him were new experiences for her, she was game for anything. Willing to try and willing to laugh at herself if things didn't work out exactly as either of them had planned.

He'd dated a lot of women in his lifetime, some of the most beautiful women in the world. But never had he felt this connection—this oneness he felt every moment of every day when he was with Contessa. She gave him a peace he had not even realized he was missing.

And when they lay together at night and he pulled her against his body, she molded against him like she was designed just for that purpose. There was nowhere he could touch her that she did not respond. And he knew it was not just his own vanity that told him she had never responded to another man like she did for him. It was also some bone-deep feeling. The same feeling that told him this was the woman he was going to spend the rest of his life with.

He was thrilled to realize she lived in Connecticut. Since he was moving back home at the end of this little mini-vacation, they could continue their relationship easily instead of trying to communicate long-distance. He started to tell her so more than once, but some instinct told him to hold off. He would save it for their last night together, he thought, and surprise her.

He stood behind her on the deck of his yacht guiding her hands as she learned how to maneuver the wheel, and he found himself daydreaming about the children they would undoubtedly one day have. Of course he couldn't just ask her to marry him now, even though he considered it. It was too soon, she needed time to get used to the idea and get used to him. It was easy to fall in love in the magical romanticism of Fiji. But he was coming to understand Contessa. And he knew she would need to spend time with him on the mainland before she would even consider it. For all her practiced nonchalance, his Contessa was a pragmatic woman. He smiled realizing he even liked that about her.

Michael didn't even try to hide what he was feeling. She may've felt he was coming on too strong, too fast, but he only had a few days to bind her to him. And he still remembered how he'd met her. She'd been trolling the bar looking for a bedmate. But what if he'd decided not to go to the bar that night? Would some other man be lying with her right now? Would some other man be plotting how to keep her in his life?

On the fourth day of their interlude, Michael awoke to cold reality. His eyes popped open but he did not move right away. He could feel the weight of Contessa's head on his stomach and had no desire to disturb her. He turned his head to stare out the window at the fish swimming by in the turquoise water. *What trouble-free lives they lived*, he thought.

In another two days he would be returning home for the first time in several years. And he was expected to take over his family's business. It would be good to be back home, to see old friends and reconnect with his dad. But since he'd deliberately avoided anything that looked like work for several years, he was doubting his ability to take over the day-to-day managing of their family's airplane manufacturing business. And this probably would've been okay. Leadership would've moved on to one of his more capable siblings. Except… He was an only child.

There were no other siblings. Which in turn meant all his father's plans and hopes and dreams were riding on his shoulders. Honestly, he didn't know if he was up to the challenge, but somehow knowing he would have Contessa at his side made it better.

They only had two more days together and, as if by silent consent, neither of them brought up the fact that they would be leaving soon, fearing an uncertain tomorrow would intrude on their little piece of heaven.

But Michael could not hide his anxiety as time went on. The closer it got to the time to leave, the more noticeably nervous he became until Contessa finally said something.

They were walking down the long corridor leading back to her suite, holding hands and walking at a leisurely pace. To anyone passing by, they would appear for all the world like a happy couple taking a stroll.

But Connie knew something was troubling Michael. She didn't know how she knew, or even what the problem may be, she just knew he was incredibly tense which was not at all like him.

"Anything you want to talk about?" she asked, glancing up at his handsome face.

He shrugged indifferently. Taking the door key from her, he opened the suite entrance and followed her in.

Contessa headed to the bedroom, her mouth pursed thoughtfully. She'd offered a sympathetic ear, and he'd said no, which meant she should leave it alone, right? She kicked off her heeled sandals and went back into the other room where he was sitting on the couch. His head was back against the cushions, he looked exhausted and her heart went out to him. She sat down beside him and took his closest hand between her own. "Tell me."

He turned his head to look at her and smiled. "You're so beautiful, you know that?"

She arched a eyebrow. "Are you trying to distract me? Come one, something is obviously bothering you."

"You remember me telling you I was from Hartford?"

"Yes, but you're currently staying in your family home in the Hamptons right?"

He nodded. "The good news is that when I leave here, I'm heading back to Hartford. The bad news is that it's to take over my family business."

She frowned. "Why isn't that a good thing?"

"Because I don't know the first thing about it."

"But you'll learn."

"Yeah, but that takes time and quite frankly, I'm not certain I will. I'm an only child and I've always known eventually I would have to do this. I guess I'm just angry with myself for not doing anything about it. I could've been preparing for this all my life, but I didn't, and now here I am at the eleventh hour wishing I knew more than I do."

She laid her head against his shoulder, still holding his large hand between her much smaller ones. "Don't do this to yourself. Would've, should've, could've never helps. All you can do at this point is move forward. When you get there, try to learn everything you can as fast as you can. And I can personally vouch for your learning curve. You'll do fine." She smiled.

"I'm just terrified I'm going to make some terrible mistake and cost the company millions of dollars during that *learning curve.*"

"Michael, I don't know him but I can't imagine your father would bring you to work for him—only child or no only child—unless he thought you could do the work. This is his company, he's spent his life building this enterprise, he's not going to knowingly put it in jeopardy."

He smiled back. "That is him to a T. I know he loves me and he loves his company, but I've never doubted the pecking order. Sure you don't know him?"

"No, but I know the type. My boss is exactly the same. The company is like a child in itself. After investing a lifetime in it, I guess it would be hard to let go. So, try to see it from his point of view."

He stared down at the carpet. "I guess you're right. He's probably more nervous than me that his life's work is going to go up in flames—sacrificed on the altar of paternal love."

She laughed. "Ready to go to bed?"

The flame of passion lit instantly. He turned his head and his eyes ran over her from top to bottom even as she stood and brought him to his feet with her. They stood, bodies pressed together and just held each other.

Contessa cupped his face in her hands. "You'll do fine."

"And of course, I'll be the boss. So, anyone who dares to point out my flaws will find themselves reassigned to *parts unknown*."

She placed a quick kiss on his lips. "See, you're already learning." She turned and still holding on to his hand, guided him to the bedroom.

Michael watched the sway of her hips as she walked away from him. He was considering changing his flight plans, so they would return together. After all, he wasn't expected back at any specific time. He found he did not want to be away from her for any length of time if possible.

As she approached the bed, he suddenly scooped her up in his arms and tossed her across the comforter. Her startled laughter did wonders for his disposition as he came down on top of her. He placed kisses in rapid succession across her face, her throat. "I can't believe I'm going to have to go without this for…how long?"

Her eyes suddenly clouded over and her smile fell away, but she quickly schooled her expression into a blank mask and Michael was left wondering what the hell had just happened. He rolled off her and propped himself up on his elbow. "Contessa? We were going to keep seeing each other, right? I mean, I thought this was more than an island fling? Is it?"

She reached up and touched his face. "Yes, most definitely yes. It's just things are not the same back home as they are here."

"What do you mean?"

"Here it's only us with no intrusions. Back home, I'll have my family, you'll have your new responsibilities. I can't see how we can maintain what we have here."

His eyes narrowed on her face. "Are you married?"

She frowned. "What?"

He sat straight up. "You heard me—are you married?"

She sat up, as well. "No, of course not. Do you think I could be here with you doing this if I were?"

He was still frowning, but the tension in his body had relaxed some. "Some women could. I didn't think you were one of them, but you never know. Is there someone else in your life?"

"No, no. Nothing like that. I'm not in any relationship or anything resembling a relationship. That's not what I'm talking about."

"Then, what's the problem? We both have feelings for the other, right?"

She nodded.

"Then, what's the hang-up?"

She shook her head. "I guess there aren't any."

His face lit in a bright smile. "Great." He lay back down on the bed, his arms folded behind his head. "We'll fly back to Connecticut and I'll build my planes and you'll…" He frowned up at the ceiling. "Hell, I don't even know what you do for a living."

The statement was met with silence. He glanced at her to find her staring at a spot on the floor as if mesmerized. "Contessa? What is it you do for a living?" She just continued to stare at the floor as if paralyzed. "Contessa?"

She jerked as if startled awake. "Huh?"

"I asked what do you do for a living."

"I'm a…I'm in business."

He frowned. "Wow, I don't think you can get much more general than that."

He watched as she licked her lips and swallowed slowly. When she turned to look at him, her eyes had a slightly wild look to them. "Michael, what's your last name?"

His eyebrows rose. "Do you mean we've been together

this whole week and neither of us has asked the other's last name? It's Hillard, by the way. What's yours?"

She bit her bottom lip and for a moment he thought she would not answer. Finally, she said. "Smith. Contessa Smith." She lay back on the bed, snuggling against his side.

Michael lay staring up at the ceiling, his mind in turmoil. If she wasn't married, why would she lie about her last name? And there was no doubt she was lying—the only comfort was that she was so lousy at it, she obviously didn't do it a lot.

A few minutes later, he turned to her, pulled her into his arms and made love to her. But afterward, instead of the feeling of contentment and satisfaction that usually followed, he felt cold and unexplainably *pushed away.*

Contessa fell asleep almost instantly, but Michael lay awake for a long while, replaying the evening in his mind. Something had changed. Something that was said or done had abruptly ended their perfect holiday even sooner than planned. But for the life of him, he could not figure out what.

Chapter 6

She was gone. He knew it even before he turned over and looked at the empty pillow next to his head. Reasonably, he knew the sense of dread he was feeling was probably a bit extreme. But there was something about the way she'd looked at him right before they fell asleep the night before, as if she were memorizing his face.

Throwing back the covers he climbed out of bed, went to the wardrobe closet and opened the doors. All that hung in there were the khaki shorts and white polo shirt he'd worn the day before. Her suitcases, all her clothes, and after a trip to the bathroom he knew her toiletries were gone, as well. They were all gone. Every sign, every bit of evidence that she'd been there was gone.

He showered and dressed in his slightly wrinkled clothes, all the while feeling as if he were weighed down by lead bars. Once he was dressed, he called the front desk and confirmed his suspicion. She had checked out early that morning.

Michael fought to control his reaction, but he felt like

screaming his denial. She'd left him. Just up and left him without so much as a goodbye. Not even so much as a note. *Why?*

He sat on the side of the bed, braced his elbows on his knees and held his head. He tried to understand. How could he have been making love to the woman of his dreams just a few hours before and now she was gone from his life? And he didn't even know where or how to find her. To his amazement and frustration, he realized that even though they had spent the week in constant conversation he'd learned very little about her.

Looking back, it was obvious that she'd been deliberately vague, but he'd been so enamored of her pretty face and fantastic body, he had not noticed the stunning lack of substance. *Why? What was she hiding?*

He considered that maybe the past week had been some kind of elaborate game. Maybe she was some kind of siren who traveled to hot vacation spots, having meaningless sex with strange men and making them fall in love with her. But no sooner had that thought formulated than he'd discarded it.

Michael had been with his fair share of women, he knew when he was being played. And truth be told, he'd done his fair share of manipulating over the years, as well. He knew beyond a doubt that what he'd experienced over the past week was real.

So... Why?

He stood and took a deep breath. First things first. He would travel to Connecticut and then work out a plan to find her. If for no other reason than to find out what had gone wrong. A troubling thought occurred to him for the first time. Maybe she wasn't even from Connecticut. Maybe she just said that because he said he was from Connecticut. But why would she do that? Nothing made any sense anymore, he thought, as he collected his wallet and keys from the nightstand and headed out of the suite. At the door, he paused and looked back over the rooms. He glanced out the glass window where the ocean life was going about its business uninterrupted. And he thought about the woman who'd resided there for the past week, the woman who'd stolen his heart. Somehow he would track her down. Somehow he would find her and get her back.

Later than day, he completely lost his resolve to get on with life. He canceled his flight, went back to his yacht and proceeded to get completely drunk. He decided there was no point in trying to find a woman who didn't want to be found.

He was Michael Hillard, dammit. There were woman falling over themselves to get into his bed. He would not demean himself by chasing down some lying little schemer just so she could see how she had rattled his world. He wouldn't give her the satisfaction.

He woke the following morning with a hangover the size of an auditorium, and spent most of the morning in bed nursing it. Thankfully, George had taken care of everything else, so he was allowed to wallow in his self-pity as long as he wanted.

By the next morning, the headache was gone but not the heartache, nor the feeling that he'd been duped. Thankfully, George asked few questions, but moved around the boat like a ghost picking up behind him, and generally making his life as comfortable as could be.

That night, he showered, shaved, dressed and headed back to Victoria Parade fully intending to find another dance partner. Someone who could wipe Contessa from his brain. But it didn't take long for him to realize it was a bad idea. Everywhere he looked he saw her beautiful, smiling face. There was no way he could enjoy this with anyone else.

The call came on the third day after Contessa had disappeared. His father, gently but firmly, questioning him about his plans. Michael agreed to head home within the next couple days without delay. Just to make sure it happened, his father told him, he was sending his private jet. And he did.

Michael left the island on schedule. After all, what was the point in staying? As he boarded the flight heading back to the U.S., Michael wondered if he would ever be able to enjoy Fiji again.

As Connie stood beside the company limousine waiting for the Hillard private jet to come to a stop on the runway, she took deep, long breaths. Her heart was racing, in part from the anticipation of seeing Michael again. It had only been a few days since she'd left the island, but it felt like months. The other part of her was fearing the possibility of seeing recognition in his eyes. What would it bring? A look of happiness in being reunited, or revulsion upon seeing her as she really was. Or maybe just confusion, given the way she had run off. Whatever his initial reaction would be, she made a vow to herself to handle it with dignity.

When she'd arrived home, her worst fears were confirmed. Michael Hillard was indeed the son of her boss, Reginald Hillard. And Reginald was expecting his son any day now to start learning the business. But it got worse in ways she never could've imagined.

Apparently, because she knew so much about the company Reginald wanted *her* to train him. Which would mean working directly with Michael one-on-one. She'd spent two sleepless nights trying to find a way out of it, and there was none short of quitting her job.

The plane finally came to a stop and the flight crew moved in to do their various jobs. She double-checked the pleat of her suit jacket. She had chosen a dark blue skirt suit that's only fashionable touch was the gold-colored buttons that lined the edge and cuffs. Her light auburn hair was darkened and knotted in a bun so tight it was pulling at her temples. Her low-heeled navy blue pumps were completely unadorned and she wore them with skin-colored panty hose. The only jewelry she wore was a pair of tiny gold studs. No makeup, no perfume. There was nothing exceptional about her appearance. This was Connie Vaughn on a typical workday.

But just as an added precaution, last week she'd bought the dark brown contacts she was now wearing, on the off chance he remembered her only distinctive feature, her hazel eyes.

She was not wearing a single item from her trip, she had packed everything into a plastic tub and pushed it under her bed. She had tried to pack her memories of the trip in there as well, but no matter how she had tried, she could not wipe away all the wonderful memories of Michael, his touch, his scent, his voice. And now those memories were encouraging her to pull the tight pins out of her hair, tear off her staid business suit and reveal her true self to Michael.

That's how she thought of her Contessa persona, as her true self. But in the world where she lived, the world of Hillard Sr., the world of her brother, Brian, and his wife, Annie, that world only knew Connie. And for their sake and hers, from now on, she would have to be Connie to Michael Hillard, as well.

Contessa would be no more.

The door on the jet opened and the stairs lowered, and she unconsciously held her breath until the man who's body she now knew as well as her own appeared in the entryway. He was more handsome than she had remembered, his close-cropped dark hair neatly cut, his chocolate-brown skin as flawless as ever. He—like she—was dressed for business. A dark-colored suit and white shirt perfectly accented by a bright red tie. His broad shoulders filled out the suit in a way padding never could. He had the regal bearing of a young prince and just looking at him broke her heart.

For the first time in the past few days, Connie was doubtful that she could succeed in keeping her identity a secret. How was she supposed to work with him everyday, day in and day out and never reveal to him who she was? Never remind him of what they had shared and seek it out again?

How was she supposed to go the rest of her life without ever lying in his arms again?

With a light jog he came down the stairs, an entourage of people behind him, including the crew. Immediately, she noticed something different about him, but she couldn't put her finger on it. He looked the same, he moved the same, but there was something....

She watched as he crossed the open area, headed toward her.

A few seconds later he was standing in front of her, looking directly at her before she quickly looked away. And in that brief moment, she saw...nothing. Not even a hint of recognition. *But that's exactly what I wanted, right?* she thought. A small part of her conscience was honest enough to admit that no, that's not what she wanted at all.

He extended his hand. "You must be Connie."

Hearing his voice again caught her slightly off guard. Like everything else about him, it was the same, yet different. She tried not to stare, but it was so good to see him again.

She took the extended hand. "Yes, I am." She spoke softer than her normal tone, hoping that together with her appearance, his brain would not recognize her voice. "Welcome back to Connecticut, Mr. Hillard. I'm supposed to escort you back directly to the office. Your father is very anxious to meet with you." She climbed inside the car and moved to the far side, but once he was in the car with her, there was nowhere she could go to get away from his overwhelming presence.

As the driver closed the door behind him, he settled on the seat across from her and leaned his head back against the cushions and closed his eyes. "Not to be rude, but it's been a really long day. Hope you don't mind if I take a little nap on the ride back to the office."

Connie frowned. She had a lot to talk to him about, and he wanted to take a nap? She could've insisted they discuss his father's itinerary for him, forced him to stay awake and talk to her. But instead she said nothing, having her own selfish reasons for wanting the silence to stand. She was still reeling from his very real lack of recognition. She knew that was a possibility, had known it all along. But still having it actually happen, looking into his eyes and seeing nothing, it stung, like nothing she'd ever felt before.

She pushed the automated button to let the window down just slightly, needing some fresh air to cool her heated body. It was just nerves she knew, but she was getting hotter by the moment.

After a few seconds, she heard soft snoring coming from the other side of the car and realized he was sound asleep. Connie took the opportunity to watch him. He really was a beautiful man, and Connie was still slightly surprised to realize this man was her lover. Would be now, if she had anything resembling a spine running along her back. He was so large, and yet such an incredibly gentle lover. Never once did she feel suffocated, or overwhelmed by his size and strength.

She let her hungry eyes run over every part of his body, remembering what he had looked like beneath that perfectly tailored suit. She remembered the insecurity in his voice when he had spoken of returning home to take up the helm of his father's business. Some part of her knew that was a piece of the strain he was currently feeling. She wished she could cross the car to his seat, put her arms around him and comfort him. Let him know the truth of his father's demand. Tell him that what he thought of as a decree was really just the yearning of a lonely man, wanting to spend more time with his only child before it was too late.

But of course, she could do none of that, because he thought they were just meeting for the first time and she would of course, know nothing of his secret fears. That was the kind of thing a man shared with his lover.

She stared out the window of the speeding car wondering when, if ever, would the desire to be with him go away? She had passed the first test, he in no way recognized her. But somehow, her first victory did not feel like a victory at all. In fact, it felt like the exact opposite of a victory.

Next, she would have to work with him on a continuing basis, and ensure that that nonrecognition continued, at least for the next few months. Then he would be ready to take on his new position and she would be allowed to return to her routine, probably only seeing him occasionally.

Eventually, the memories of Fiji and the wonderfully sexy and vibrant man she had met there would fade and be replaced by the suited-up businessman sitting across from her right now. At least that was what she was hoping.

It took almost an hour to drive back to the company headquarters outside of Hartford. He woke up shortly before they arrived, glanced at her briefly, apologized again for sleeping on the ride and turned his attention to staring out the window until they pulled up in the drive.

Silently, Connie sent him whatever strength she could, knowing that he was thinking about the upcoming meeting with his father. After all, it had been several months since the two had even seen each other, and as far as she knew they had never actually worked together.

Here she was thinking about her little problems, forgetting Michael had his own fears to contend with. She knew that it would be okay. After all, unlike him, she had worked with his father every day and knew how much the man was looking forward to having his son back. She knew that Michael could turn out to be the worst airplane contractor in the history of the world and he would still succeed in his father's eyes. But this would have to be something he discovered on his own.

As they pulled up in front of the rectangular-shaped chrome-colored building, Michael leaned forward to get a better look.

"Very nice." He nodded, and glanced back at Connie. "I

haven't been back to Connecticut since the new headquarters were built."

Connie did a quick calculation in her head, the building was built over seven years ago, they had moved in over six years ago. She knew Michael and his father often met at their vacation home in the Hamptons, but she did not realize it had been so long since Michael had been back to his home state. Connie had wondered why in all the years she'd worked for Reginald Hillard, she'd never met his son, even in passing. Now she knew why.

"We have a complete test facility right on-site now, so we no longer have to send out for prototyping. It makes the whole process much faster."

He glanced back at her and chuckled. "He's come a long way from the first building in New London." He smiled, and suddenly she was transported back to the island. Connie thought she would melt right there on the seat.

Instead she held her emotions in check, and gave a small smile. "I've seen the pictures."

"Trust me, the pictures do not do it justice. It was like a rat resort, they were everywhere." He laughed. "It was so bad, he wouldn't even bring potential clients there. He had a small showroom set up on the other side of town and he would take them there."

"Everyone has to start somewhere." She tried not to stare, but his good humor felt so warm and familiar, she had not realized how much she had missed his laughter until now.

"Yes, you're right. And if there is one thing my father has, it's determination to succeed."

"You have that same quality."

He gave her a slightly confused look, and Connie realized her mistake. "At least that's what your father told me."

She shrugged, and his smile faded. "I guess we will see, won't we?"

His lack of confidence was so apparent it was heartbreaking, but Connie did not know what to say without sounding like a complete idiot.

"The first order of business is I'm supposed to give you a complete tour of the facility," Connie said, as the car pulled to a stop and the chauffeur came around to open the door.

Michael frowned. "Didn't you say my father was anxious to see me?"

She nodded. "Yes, but he's in a meeting until three."

He glanced at his watch. "Maybe I should just head to the house."

Now she frowned. "You don't want to see the facility?"

He glanced out the window once more. "No, not now." His eyes darted to hers. "Could you arrange a tour at another time? I'm just really tired coming off this trip."

Connie sensed something else was going on, but again she could not really ask without coming off as super-intrusive.

"Would this time tomorrow be good for you?"

"Perfect." He reached over and placed his hand on her arm, and Connie felt the touch all the way to her toes. "I really appreciate your working with me."

She smiled and pushed up her glasses on her nose. "That's what I'm here for." As she climbed out of the car, she called back. "I'll let your father know."

The door was closed and a few seconds later she watched the rear of the car as it turned off the drive and merged back into the business traffic of the main throughway. She stood there for a few minutes replaying the afternoon in her head.

The good news was that Michael Hillard had no idea that she was his island lover and would therefore make no attempts to pick up where they had left off.

The bad news was…that Michael Hillard had no idea she was his island lover and would therefore make no attempts to pick up where they had left off.

Chapter 7

As the limo pulled into the long gravel driveway leading to the colonial brick house that rose up before them, Michael leaned out the window. He had not been here since he was a teenager.

It wasn't that he had bad memories of the place. In fact, it was just the opposite. This was the place where his mother's memory lived. This was the place where he had celebrated the happiest holidays of his life, experienced the most significant moments of a young man's life. It was where he grew to be a man nestled in the bosom of loving parents. This was home.

Now after years of bouncing between their family's various other homes, he was back, and at first glance, time seemed to have stood still.

The door to the car opened and he stood beside it, continuing to take in the perfectly manicured grounds and pristine house. He'd expected to feel a lot of things coming here, and a feeling of satisfaction was not supposed to top the list, but it did.

Actually being here, he could now see that at some point over the years a sense of peace had settled around the loss of his mother. As the beloved only child of Madeline Hillard, Michael had bathed in her love and attention during his early life. Her sudden loss as the result of a heart attack had left him devastated and he'd grieved for a long time.

But now, being in the home he'd shared with her and his father, the pain wasn't nearly as sharp as he'd expected. He was healing, and now knew he could stay here without being haunted by a ghost of the past.

As the driver took his bags from the trunk, Michael went up the steps and the front door swung open. The middle-aged man who answered the door smiled in greeting.

Michael did not recognize him, but smiled in return anyway.

"Welcome, Mr. Hillard. My name is Carl. I'm your father's personal assistant."

Michael stopped himself from shaking his head. An assistant at the office, one at home. He was surprised his father didn't have one just for the car.

"Nice to meet you, Carl."

Carl closed the front door after the driver set Michael's bags on the foyer floor inside the house. Michael had walked over to look up the stairs, at the walls lining the stairwell, still surprised by how little had changed over the years.

Carl picked up the bags and climbed the stairs. "I'll just carry these to your room." And he disappeared, moving at a speed Michael wouldn't have thought possible, based on the age of the man.

Michael decided to take a few minutes to familiarize himself with his home. He wandered around the lower floor, from the dining room through the kitchen, the great room and finally out to the terrace that lined the back of the house. Even the little knickknacks scattered throughout the rooms had not changed, including childish odds and ends he'd created over the years, and handed out as gifts to his mother, still lined the shelves.

He'd missed the place, more than he had realized. He should've come back sooner but a part of him feared what he would find here. But today, even not knowing how he would react to being back, he knew he had to come and face it. Contessa had taught him that.

Leaning against the metal railing that lined the terrace, Michael stared out over the lawn, letting his mind wander back to the woman who had consumed his thoughts for the past few days. He'd made a conscious decision not to dwell on a woman that had abandoned him. But at that moment, he desperately wanted her by his side.

He wished he could talk to her about what he was feeling. He knew she would understand. She had a way of knowing what he was thinking and feeling even before he said it. She knew what he wanted even before he asked. A talent that was especially wonderful in a lover.

But she wasn't there. She knew who he was, she knew where to find him. Some part of him still hoped that she would come looking for him. Some part of him still hoped there was some explanation. He hadn't received so much as a phone call.

For all the evidence he had of their interlude, she could've been a figment of his imagination. And as much as he hated to admit it, he had finally begun to accept that maybe she had left because she was simply done with him. That what had been a life-altering experience for him, had just been a casual affair for her.

The cynic in him thought maybe it was just karma. As a man who'd spent most of his adult life fighting off marriage-minded women, now when he finally found one he wanted to marry, she would disappear like mist. Was he just getting what he was owed?

Not that it mattered. Not now. Not anymore. She didn't want him, that was plain enough, and he would just have to find a way to get over that hurt and move on. He had to devote his mind and attention to learning the family business. His father was right. It was high time he take on some serious responsibility. He only hoped he could rise to the challenge.

Although he'd only spoken to her a moment, it was obvious his father's assistant, Connie, knew her stuff. She spoke with a kind of pride that came from someone invested in what she was doing, and he would probably do good to learn as much as he could from her. His father sung her praises, and that alone was a telling sign. Reginald Hillard was not a man who was easy to please, but he was willing to pay well for exceptional performance. The woman was the picture of competence in her mall-store business suit.

His cell phone rang. He pulled it from his pocket and answered. "Hello?"

"Michael? Connie said you went straight home, everything okay?"

"Hi, Dad. Yes, I'm fine, just a little wiped out."

"Any problems with the flight?"

"No, no, everything was fine. Thanks for sending the jet for me."

"I'm just glad you're finally home, son. Did you have any plans for later? I wanted to take you to dinner."

"No, no plans. Dinner sounds great."

"Good. I have a couple more things to do and then I'll be right along. In the meantime, just let Carl know if you need anything."

"All right, I'll be here."

"Son, it's good to have you home."

"It's good to be back home." Michael was surprised to find, even as he said the words, that they were true.

* * *

As he hung up the phone, Reginald Hillard smiled up at his assistant.

Connie smiled back. "See, I told you he was okay."

"Right as always, my dear. I just needed to hear his voice." He patted her hand where it rested on his desk next to his. His face wrinkled in concern. "I just wish I didn't have all these damn meetings over the next few days, but there was no way around it. And it's really pointless to bring him into the meetings until he has a better understanding of the day-to-day functions." He spun his swivel chair around to face her. "You'll take care of him for me, won't you, Connie? Take him around, show him the ropes?"

Connie nodded and busied herself with the files scattered around his desk. "Of course, Mr. Hillard. I'll bring him up to speed just as we discussed. Is there anything you want to add to the list?"

He shook his head thoughtfully. "No, just the items we discussed. Don't want to overwhelm him." He sat back in his chair. "You know, I'm asking you to do this not just because you have such a proficient knowledge of the company, but there is another reason."

Connie's hands stilled while holding a stack of papers from his desk. "Another reason?" she asked cautiously.

He nodded firmly. "Yes. Connie, you love this company almost as much as I do—I want you to convey that sense of pride to him, if that is at all possible."

She smiled at the man who had become like a father or an uncle to her over the years. "I doubt if that is even necessary, Mr. Hillard. I'm sure your son already loves this company every bit as much as you do." She finished organizing his desk and headed back to hers which sat just outside the larger suite.

Connie loved her job. She'd been hired into the secretarial pool ten years ago, and through hard work and late hours—

mostly done as a way to avoid going home to Nathan whe
she was married, and then Brian and Annie when she ha
moved in with them—she'd worked her way up to executiv
assistant to the president of the company.

And no one could ask for a better boss than Reginald Hi
lard. He was demanding, but fair. And Connie had not bee
looking forward to the possibility that she would have to leav
the company if things became awkward between her and M
chael. But if his reaction today was any indication, she ha
nothing to worry about. There was nothing in his demeanc
or speech to indicate that the past week had represented any
thing significant in his life. It had changed her world foreve.
Now, thanks to the confidence she had gained, she was read
to get her own place. What had seemed like enough was n
longer. There was so much to life, so much living to do an
she wanted to do it. She had conceded defeat too quickly be
fore but, thanks to Michael, she knew what victory felt like—
and she wanted more. What that meant exactly, or how sh
was to go about getting it, was still a mystery. But nonethe
less, for her, the past week had changed her whole world an
it was all thanks to Michael Hillard.

As for him, he just looked like a man recovering from a
island fling.

Chapter 8

As he stood at the large windows facing out of his expansive corner office, Michael could not shake the feeling that his life would forever be divided into two parts. Pre-Contessa and now post-Contessa.

Before he had met the woman, he'd been a man perfectly content with his lot in life. *Hell,* more than content. He'd spent his youth living every playboy's dreams, and in the company of some of the most beautiful women in the world. And now only one woman would do. And no matter how he tried to pick up the pieces and move on, it was impossible.

At first he'd convinced himself that his current state of unhappiness was due to the way in which she'd ended their affair. Sneaking out without so much as a goodbye. But now, weeks later, he was left with nothing but the truth. When she had left the island, she had taken his heart with her.

For the first time in his life, Michael Hillard was experiencing a broken heart—and it hurt like hell. But worse than the pain of never knowing what could've been, was not know-

ing why. Why she'd left him the way she did. He knew she
felt something for him, maybe not love, but enough to, at the
very least, exchange real phone numbers.

At the soft knock at the door, he turned slightly to see Connie crossing the room with a manila folder extended toward
him. "You father asked me to discuss this account with you.
Do you have a moment?"

Michael glanced at her bowed head, as she studied her
every step, to the extended arm and back to her bowed head.
It just occurred to him that he'd worked with the woman for
almost a month now and had no idea what color her eyes
were. She always walked with her head down as if fearing
she would fall if she was not constantly vigilant.

"Sure." He took the file and opened it to find it contained
information on a new design for one of their biggest clients.

In the weeks he'd been there, he'd spent most of his time
learning about the inner workings of the company itself. He'd
been given a complete "how to" course of their finance department. Plus a guided tour of both their local plants and
planned future tours of the various locations around the world.
And although it was not necessary, a complete rundown of
the Hillard family history and how the company had come
to be. All thanks to his father's obsessively competent assistant. She might not be much for eye-to-eye contact, but she
was one hell of a right-hand man.

Despite the long hours and busy schedule, Michael had always known that was filler work until he found his footing.
He'd always assumed his father did not bring him out of his
quasi-hiatus just to count beans. And the file in his hands
now confirmed his belief. This was a major project for one
of their biggest contracts. Unlike most of what he'd done so
far, this was important. And Michael understood it was also
his father's way of saying it was time to get down to business.

True to the established pattern of the past few weeks, when
a task was important, his father placed it into the hands of his

most trusted employee. This explained why Connie Vaughn was standing in front of him counting carpet threads.

With her hands at her sides, and her head downcast, she looked like a child about to be scolded. Michael pretended to review the file as he let his eyes roam over the petite woman, wondering why she dressed in such dowdy clothes when she obviously had a pretty decent figure underneath all those sweaters and high-collared blouses.

And she always wore her auburn hair in that tight bun at the back of her head, which was a shame really because even in the dim light of the office, her golden highlights were noticeable. Michael thought it was kinda strange how some women like Contessa just had a natural sense of style as to what made them look best, and other women, like Connie, could barely match their socks. With the right coaching, it was obvious Connie had a lot of potential to be an attractive woman. Too bad she didn't have someone like Contessa to show her how to accent her best features.

"Are you familiar with the 160 Airbus?" A small finger came over the top of the file to point to a line. "It's a new design, but we fully expect it to be one of our best sellers."

He nodded. "Yes, Dad said something about it last year. But weren't there some design problems with it?"

She nodded eagerly. "Were. We've fixed all the major problems." She moved to his side and began turning pages in the file. "See, here and here. The heavy wing issue here."

He resisted the urge to turn his head in her direction knowing if he looked directly at her, she would scurry away from him with the speed of an urban squirrel.

"Yes, but wasn't there also some kind of problem with the rotors?"

She glanced up at his face, but when he held her gaze, her eyes—light brown—went wide in amazement. What? Did she think he was an idiot?

"Yes, that's right. But you see here—" she turned a couple

pages "—it was just a calculation problem. Once we knew what the problem was, it was an easy fix."

He gestured to his small, round conference table in the corner of the office. "Let's sit down. So, since all the major issues have been resolved, what am I supposed to be doing here?"

As they reached the table, she pulled a chair over closer to the one he'd chosen to sit in. Sitting down beside him, she reached for the folder and turned back to the first page. "Well, you need to review the file, and let me know if you have any other concerns regarding the design, then we move into the prototype stage of production."

"Who pays for that?"

"We do initially and back bill it to the customer once they accept the design."

Michael reclined in his chair and looked directly at her. "Can I ask you a personal question?" He watched as her whole body tensed in response.

"Yes?"

"Well, you're obviously more than capable of doing this job, so why don't you?"

"What do you mean?" She fussed with the folder to avoid looking at him, but Michael was not fooled and thought maybe he was beginning to understand.

"I mean, I can't imagine my father being the astute businessman I know him to be letting a talent like yours go wasted."

She looked up at him, directly at him for the first time and although she was frowning, Michael had the sudden feeling of déjà vu. He doubted that she'd actually frowned at him before, since she barely looked at him at all. But still, something about her frown bothered him.

He smiled at her in return. His million-dollar-playboy smile, the one that had served him well over his twenty-seven years.

Apparently, she was immune because her frown intensified. "What do you mean *wasted?*"

His smiled faded, as he realized his mistake. "I didn't mean what you do is not important."

"Then what do you mean?"

"It's just that you can do so much more. I mean, you know as much about this company as I do."

She started to say something and given the ongoing frown, Michael knew it would not be anything good. But instead, something in her shifted, and she suddenly became extremely self-conscious and looked down again.

"Thank you," she mumbled. "I'll take that as a compliment." Using her index finger, she absently pushed up her glasses.

Now Michael frowned wondering what had just happened. He quickly replayed the two-minute conversation in his head and immediately understood that because of his careless insult, little Miss Ultra Control lost it—only for an instant—but it was long enough for the curtain to drop and for Michael to like what he saw behind it.

When she wasn't working so hard to be meek and timid, she was actually, kinda...well, kinda interesting. She apparently had opinions, one of which was a sense of pride in her job. He would have to remember that for the future.

Suddenly, she stood. "Well, just let me know if there are any other changes you feel necessary and I'll make them right away."

"Is there a deadline on this?"

"Thursday by three, if possible?"

He nodded, sitting back in his chair looking up at her. "Look, sorry if what I said was in any way offensive. I truly meant it as a compliment."

She flashed a smile. "I know. Thank you." She turned and scurried across the room to the door, and as she pulled it closed behind her, Michael was once again left with a feeling of déjà vu. This made no sense whatsoever.

Connie hurried down the hall with her arms wrapped around her midsection, her heart racing in her chest. She was starting to get used to the excitement she felt whenever she managed to get away from him without him realizing who she was.

And this time was more thrilling than the others, because she was certain she'd seen a spark of recognition in his eyes— just for a moment, but she was almost certain it had been real. If he did, it was her own fault. Over the past couple weeks, she'd become lax in keeping up her disguise and did not always wear her contacts, like today. She couldn't let that happen again.

Her mind was racing so that she turned a corner and almost ran into the mail cart sitting unattended in a hallway, but caught herself just in time. From the moment she'd left Michael in Fiji, Connie had been torn. Her mind thought she was doing the right thing, the only thing she could do. But her heart was another matter. Standing so close to him, smelling his wonderful scent, hearing his deep voice resonate around her. And now, knowing how intelligent he was, experiencing how his brain worked. She was finding that the more she knew about him, the more she loved him when in fact just the opposite was supposed to be happening.

He was supposed to reveal himself for the shallow, self-conceited playboy she'd convinced herself he was. He was supposed to be trifling and useless, and eventually she would come to see his true nature and stop loving him. Right?

But instead, he was turning out to be more wonderful than she could've ever imagined, with levels of depth she had never even considered. How was she supposed to stop loving him when he was becoming more lovable by the day?

Somehow, she would have to, because there was simply no

way they could be together again. Not like they were before, and Connie could never settle for less. Although, Connie held no illusions that Michael would even want to continue their relationship if he knew who she really was. After all, she'd presented a false front. Contessa and Connie may occupy the same body, but beyond that they had nothing in common.

That night, Michael had a disturbing dream. It was about Contessa, as most of his dreams had been lately. But instead of the lust-fueled visions he'd had before, this dream was closer to a nightmare. She was racing down a hallway, wearing the black dress and spiky heels she'd been wearing the night he had met her. It took a moment to recognize where they were, but it was the corridor right outside his office. He was chasing her and every once in a while she would glance back over her shoulder at him with a look of pure terror on her face. He couldn't understand why she was so scared… of him? What had he ever done to make her afraid of him?

He ran and ran, reaching out for her but could never quite grab hold of her. He followed her around the corner at the end of the corridor and found himself in the main lobby of the building. Contessa had simply disappeared. In the middle of the marble floor of the lower level was a desk and sitting at the desk was Connie, his father's assistant.

She was busy at work, and did not even look up from her work as he hurried past still looking for some sign of his Contessa. Realizing Contessa was nowhere to be found, he turned to Connie to ask her if she'd seen Contessa, but strangely he found himself looking right at Contessa. She was plainer than he was used to seeing her, but it was Contessa's hazel eyes staring back at him. Contessa's beautiful smile on Connie's face. Contessa's eyes and smile…but Connie's face?

Michael's eyes opened and he sat straight up in the bed.

Chapter 9

He stood leaning against the wall a few feet away. Her back was to him and he was certain she did not know he was there. He wished he could move around to get a better look at her face. But that would alert her to his presence. And for now he just wanted to be able to watch her uninterrupted.

It was just a dream. He'd repeated that same phrase over and over and yet he was still standing here. Watching her body movement, looking for any sign of the woman he loved. And yes, against all odds he still loved her. *But, there was no way it was possible.*

He'd worked with this woman for the past month and there had been no sign of Contessa. *Just look at the way she dresses,* he thought. His Contessa wouldn't be caught dead in such dowdy clothes. And why would Contessa not speak to him? Not tell him who she was, even if he did not instantly recognize her?

But, it would also make sense in some strange way. It would explain the look on her face the night before she had left. When she had asked him for his last name. She would've known then that he was the son of her boss. And if she had never intended to see him again, which apparently she did not, then knowing they would soon meet again would've been alarming for her.

But how long did she think she could keep up such a charade? Well, he conceded, she'd managed to keep it up for a month so far. Maybe she thought she was free and clear. And maybe she would've been if he hadn't had that dream.

Finally, he pushed off from the wall and walked around to the front of the desk. "Good morning, Connie."

She turned in her seat and looked up at him and he stopped in his tracks. How the hell had he not seen it? With her head turned at a slight angle he could see the edge of a contact lens covering her pupil. He would bet his life that the eyes beneath the contacts were a much lighter color…hazel-gold to be exact. How could he have been this close to her this long and not realize who she was?

"Good morning, Mr. Hillard." She pushed up her glasses on her nose and continued typing.

Michael stood staring at the top of her head trying to figure what was wrong with her hair. It was much too dark. Contessa's hair had been a softer auburn color with blond highlights, which perfectly suited her caramel complexion. But Connie's hair was much, much darker, almost black in fact. Not that it mattered, he thought. There was no longer any doubt in his mind.

He just didn't know what to do with the knowledge now that he had it. Should he just walk away and allow her the privacy that she so obviously wanted? She had apparently moved on from him, so should he not just simply move on from her?

But still, a part of him wanted answers. A part of him wanted to know if he'd just imagined the feelings they had had for each other. Or maybe they had all been on his side.

Either way, he wanted to know for sure. So he could let go of her once and for all.

After several minutes, she stopped typing and looked up at him again. "Is there something I can help you with this morning, Mr. Hillard?"

He just shook his head, staring at her face intently. Her eyes widened slightly, but she quickly recovered. *That's right, dammit, I'm on to you.*

Once again, she up pushed her glasses on her nose and resumed her typing. He stood there for several more minutes, but finally walked away.

His instinct was to grab her up out of that chair and demand she tell him the truth. But the why, that terrible unanswered *why* still haunted him. And until he had a better understanding of her motives, he didn't want to strip away her mask.

For all he knew, there could be a very good reason for why she kept her true self hidden from him. For the present, he would hold his peace, but for how much longer? If she knew he was catching on, maybe now she would come to him and explain.

He could only hope. He turned and headed back to his office. Although he didn't know how he was suppose to get any work done knowing his Contessa was sitting just a few feet away, pretending for all the world as if she'd never laid eyes on him before he had stepped off the plane a month ago.

He stopped short right outside his office as another thought occurred to him. Contessa…Connie. He shook his head, once again amazed by his level of denseness.

Connie held her breath until she heard his office door shut and then exhaled. *Damn.*

She grabbed her purse from a drawer and headed toward the elevators. She needed to get out of here for a few minutes to pull herself together. She saw it, the recognition in his eyes. He knew. *Damn. Damn. Damn.*

She pushed the button on the elevator again and rung her hands nervously. How much did he know? Did he just think it was a very strong resemblance? Did he think she might be Contessa? Or did he know for certain? And if so, what did he plan to do with the information?

A month ago, she would've hazarded a guess, but the Michael Hillard who was quickly becoming a shrewd businessman was so different from her playboy lover. They could almost be two different men. Just as she was two different women.

Where the hell is the elevator? She pushed the button one more time before finally giving up and taking the stairs down. As soon as she stepped outside, a breeze blew across her face and she took a deep breath. She could breathe again.

Should she say something to him? Should she confess? Would he hate her? Would he want to pick up where they had left off? How did she think she could carry on the charade forever without him finally figuring it out?

As she crossed the street and headed to the small coffee shop, she wondered briefly, how had he figured it out? What had given her away?

She bought a chocolate chip muffin and cup of coffee and sat down at a booth in front of the window. Even if he did want to pick up where they had left off, how could they? There was the problem of how she had ended the relationship. She didn't see him forgiving her easily for running away from him. And there was the problem of her life.

She'd come back from Fiji feeling like a new woman and she'd made affirmations to change her life. But once she was settled back in her little room in Brian's house, she reverted to obedient Connie. She tried raising the possibility of getting her own place one night over dinner and Brian had shot it down like a duck during hunting season.

When he had finished quoting the crime statistics for single women living on their own, she had been almost afraid to leave the house ever again. As much as she hated to admit it, he had a point. She knew nothing about living on her own. She was thirty years old and had never lived by herself. Never established her own utilities, paid her own rent, bought her own groceries. She'd never done any of the things most women her age had. And she was terrified that if it came down to it, she would not be able to handle her own affairs. It was a depressing thought.

Connie was so different from Contessa, she was beginning to believe she'd been possessed by some sassy ghost during that wonderful week in Fiji. Contessa would've told Brian what he could do with his statistics. Connie had sat meekly and let him bully her. Although *bully* probably wasn't the right word. He was trying to help her after all.

An hour later, her nerves were settled enough for her to return to work. She only hoped that Michael's decision not to confront her directly was possibly his attempt to let sleeping dogs lie. But of course, she should've known better.

It started shortly after lunch. She felt a presence, turned to see Michael standing directly behind her. He had a strange smile on his face. No… It was actually more like a smirk.

"Did you want something, Mr. Hillard?" she asked.

"Yes, I did Ms. Smi—I mean, Ms. Vaughn, but it can wait." He turned and headed back to his office.

She pursed her lips wondering what the hell that was about. She shook her head and returned to her work. The more time that passed the less tense she was feeling.

Regardless of what Michael decided to do, she was beginning to doubt it would affect her relationship with Mr. Hillard Sr. as Junior wasn't likely to admit where he knew her from.

Throughout the rest of the day, Michael would pass her

desk giving her dirty looks, to the point where she got tired of the ill-treatment and started giving dirty looks back.

Two days later, Michael brought in a couple dozen doughnuts and a dozen muffins for the office workers. At first, Connie thought it might be some kind of peace offering as she crowded around the boxes with the rest of the people on her floor. Until she glanced over the selection and noticed something strange, just as someone else was exclaiming on the fact.

"Is this national cranberry month?" Jon from IT commented to much laughter as he settled on a cranberry muffin.

Looking over the box, Connie realized every doughnut and muffin contained some variation of cranberries. She was allergic to cranberries, a fact which she had told Michael when he had attempted to order drinks that first night they had met.

Too bad, she thought. She'd run late that morning and did not have breakfast. She could've really went for a doughnut. Connie turned to walk away from the pastry boxes and saw Michael leaning against the doorway of his office watching her, wearing a sarcastic grin. She really wanted to stride over there and knock the smirk right off his face.

Instead she walked to her desk without a word. A second later, in her peripheral vision, she saw Michael go back into his office. Up until that moment, she'd been feeling a little guilty about how things had ended between them. But now… now, he was starting to get on her *last* nerve.

The next day, she found a box on her desk. Scribbled across the top of the box read: *I remember how much you like crab legs—hope you enjoy.*

She stood looking down at the box, almost afraid to open it. She glanced around, but there was no sign of him.

Slowly, she opened the box to find a pile of steamed crab legs just as promised. But after the little trick he'd played with the doughnuts, Connie was not inclined to trust him. So, she tossed the crab legs in the garbage and returned to work.

A hour later, she practically jumped off her seat when a voice behind her shouted, "You threw them away!"

He was standing over her garbage can, where the partially open box of crab legs lay discarded. "I drove all the way to Bridgeport for that!"

"Why?"

He frowned. "Because you love crab legs and I was told that place was the best in the state."

"Let me get this straight." She folded her arms over her chest and narrowed her eyes at him. "You buy cranberry muffins so I *can't* have any, and then drive an hour one way to bring me crab legs because you know I *love* them?"

He looked away. "I felt bad about the cranberry muffin thing."

She studied him. "Are we ever going to talk about this?"

All expression fell from his face. "Discuss what?"

Connie didn't know if she should plead ignorance as well, or try to get everything brought out into the open. Instead, she just shook her head and turned around in her seat and went back to work. The man was the most trying human being she'd ever met. She glanced down at the pile of wasted crab legs and sighed in disappointment.

Obviously, she thought, he was having conflicting emotions regarding her. But, she smiled to herself glancing at the crab legs again, at least he did still have feelings for her.

Chapter 10

Their silent war got progressively worse to the point where it gained Reginald Hillard's attention. He walked into his son's office one afternoon and quietly closed the door behind him.

Michael looked up and smiled, but the smile quickly fell away when he saw the look on his father's face. "Something wrong, Dad?"

"Most certainly." He walked over to stand before the desk. "Son, I'm not an idiot. I know what you've been doing for the past several years, how you've been living your life. And I'm not condemning you. I've enjoyed my fair share of running around in my youth. But now you are in a professional workplace. More importantly a workplace where everyone looks to you to set the example. So, all those old ways of yours must come to an end."

"What are you talking about, Dad?"

"This thing with Connie. I know she's an attractive woman, son." He frowned. "Although, I daresay, I never would've imagined her being *your type*. But I won't have you making her workplace an uncomfortable environment. She's a wonderful young woman, and a excellent assistant. I won't have you mistreating her."

He shot out of his chair. "Did she tell you I mistreated her?"

"No, no." He held up his hands defensively. "But only a blind man would not see the sparks in the air every time you two pass within a few feet of each other." He coughed into his hand. "Now, it's pretty obvious she's spurned your advances, so you'll just have to take the defeat and walk away."

"What if I told you that she is the one who mistreated me?"

"You expect me to believe that?" He tilted his head to the side. "Come now. We both know Connie wouldn't hurt the feelings of a fly."

"Maybe not Connie, but Contessa would."

Reginald arched an eyebrow. "You do understand that Connie is short for Contessa. It's a nickname. They're the same wo—"

"I know! Never mind!" he snapped, and immediately regretted it. He took a deep breath. "I'm sorry, Dad. I'll try to *restrain* myself in the future."

Reginald nodded in satisfaction. "Thank you, son. I know this was an awkward conversation but it had to be done." He turned and headed back out of the room. "I'm sure once you're settled in, you'll get out and meet some women who would be more than happy to accept your advances," his father offered by way of support before opening and closing the door again.

Michael sank back down in his seat. His father was right about one thing. Something had to give. They couldn't just keep going the way things were.

He picked up the phone and dialed her extension.

"Yes, Mr. Hillard?"

"Can you come in here for a moment?"

There was a long pause, and only then did he realize they had not been alone together in his office since he'd discovered her true identity. Also, she had made sure she brought

documents to him either when she had caught him in the hall-
ways, or when he was out of his office.

"I'll be right there."

She entered the office a few seconds later and he noted the
small differences that had occurred in her appearance over
the past few days. She'd stopped using the oil on her hair and
now he could clearly see the auburn coloring he recognized
so easily. Her clothing was still rather staid by Contessa's
standard, but for Connie the mustard-colored pantsuit was
actually an improvement. At least it was a color, and not the
black and grays she'd worn those first thirty days. She had
looked like she was in mourning.

She stopped a few feet away from him, pushed up her
glasses on her nose and clasped her hands in front of her.
"Yes?"

Michael stood and slowly walked around the desk. He
folded his arms over his chest and leaned back against the
desk. "First, I want to apologize if I have in some way offended you. My father seems to think I have."

She said nothing. Just continued to stand there like a prim
little statue.

"I want to ask you a question. One question and then I will
leave you alone and say nothing else about what happened
between us in Fiji. Are you willing to answer one question
for me?"

"Depends on the question."

"All right. I—" He held up one finger and walked over
to close the door. Two workers had passed the door trying
to peer in, and Michael was forced to admit that maybe his
interest in Connie Vaughn had not gone unnoticed after all.

He returned to where he was standing before. "I just want
to know why."

"Why, what?" She frowned.

"Why did you run away from me the way you did? I

thought we were enjoying each other's company. At the risk of sounding cliché, I thought we had something special."

But she was still staring at him and said nothing, and Michael was beginning to believe he would never get his question answered.

She sank down in a nearby chair and sighed heavily. "Did you know you are only the second man I've ever been with?"

Michael could not stop his startled response. "Really?"

She nodded. "That trip to Fiji was the first time I had taken a vacation in my adult life."

Just as he'd schooled his features into indifference, his eyebrow shot up again. "Seriously?"

She nodded again. "For thirty years I've been Connie Vaughn. And for the most part, I'm okay with that." She leaned forward in her chair. "But, for just one week, I wanted to be someone else. Can you understand that?"

His eyes watched her face intensively. "I think so." He noticed she was wringing her hands. He considered reaching over to take them in his own, but he was afraid to interrupt her, fearing that once she stopped, she wouldn't start up again.

"It took me a long time, but I finally worked up a courage reserve. Unfortunately, my reserve was only for one week and it didn't include meeting someone like you."

He frowned, and found himself interrupting anyway. "What do you mean? A courage reserve?"

She was still wringing her hands and staring at the floor. "I'm not brave. Nor am I bold."

"What are you talking about? I spent a week watching you be both those things."

She shook her head. "No, that was Contessa."

"You're Contessa."

She sighed. "I know. In theory, I know. But it takes courage to be Contessa and I only had a week's reserve and that did not include falling in love."

He kneeled on the floor in front of her and took her hands

in his. "Sweetheart, I love you. More than I ever imagined loving a woman. But what you just said…" He shook his head. "That's a cop-out."

Her head shot up to his and he smiled as he watched her bite her tongue and glare at him. She probably wanted to let fly some unflattering explicatives, but for some reason she was convinced that she had to play this role that didn't even fit her.

"You don't know what it's like," she said, still glaring.

"You're right, I don't." He lifted her hands and kissed the back of one of them. "But I know you, probably better than anyone else. I got to see the real you for a whole week, and while you've got everybody fooled into believing you're this meek, humble little thing, I know the truth."

"What truth is that?"

"That you are spirited and argumentative and adventurous."

She shook her head. "No, I'm not."

He stood. "Maybe you're not. Maybe you really are the mousy little thing you claim to be. But, if that's the case, then I have to separate you from Contessa in my mind. Because my Contessa is wonderfully daring, incredibly passionate and beautiful from the inside out. I'm going to miss her…desperately. At one point I was hoping to spend my life with her."

Her head shot up and she stared wide-eyed at him.

"But if you insist on being the woman you've always been, I can't stop you." He walked around the desk and reached in the top drawer and took out a key ring.

He walked back around the desk even as he was continuing to talk. "But, if you see Contessa, can you give her this for me?"

She took the key frowning. "What is this for?"

"It's the spare key to my new apartment. If you happen to see my Contessa, tell her I miss her." He reached forward and cupped her chin in his hand. "Tell her I love her and I want her to come home to me. Will you do that for me?"

A single tear spilled onto his hand, and with three swift moves, Michael had her on her feet, in his arms and his hot mouth was coming down on her.

Chapter 11

Connie climbed the stairs leading to her front door with the reluctance of a prisoner about to be executed. If someone had told her three months ago that she would be here now, and considering doing what she was considering doing she would've never believed them. But in truth, looking back, she realized this day had been a long time coming.

She'd spent her entire life hiding her true self from the people she should've felt most comfortable around. She'd tried to please everyone but herself, and that was no kind of life.

Those few glorious days in Fiji had given her a taste of the world, a taste of happiness and satisfaction just as she'd known it would. Her only mistake was believing that would be enough. Thinking that she could just go back to being the people pleaser she'd always been, and continue to suppress her own desires. Her own dreams. And maybe she would have been able to if things had gone according to plan. If she hadn't met Michael Hillard. But in retrospect, no part of her regretted meeting Michael. Not one little bit.

She pulled her key from her purse and, taking a deep breath, she pushed open the door. After her earlier phone call to Brian, where she revealed the details of her trip and relationship with Michael, she knew he'd be upset. As she started past the living room entrance, out of her peripheral vision she could see Brian and Annie sitting on the couch together. She started to continue walking, to try and put off the confrontation as long as possible. But instead she stopped. It was time to stop being a coward.

She turned to face them and for the first time, she noticed things about her brother and his wife. Things she'd paid little, if any, attention to before. Like the way they always sat together, side by side, but rarely had she ever seen them touch, or show any signs of open affection, for that matter.

She noticed the determined and angry glint in Brian's eyes, but Annie just looked resigned. No…Connie realized, it wasn't resignation. She'd always assumed that was it, but now looking at Annie, she just looked…defeated.

Connie wondered, for the first time, how many arguments had the couple had because of her? Annie had always been her staunch advocate, and Connie had just taken that support for granted. But now, looking at them through the eyes of a woman in love, she understood that she had unknowingly put a strain on their relationship. How many times had they argued about some matter involving her? How long had they stayed up nights before this arguing?

Connie wanted to rush across the room and apologize to her sister-in-law, to tell her how much she truly appreciated her and thought of her as a true sister. But first, Connie had to deal with Brian.

She had only taken two steps into the room before Brian sprang to his feet. "I want you out!"

Connie stopped suddenly, as her eyes widened in surprise.

"If you cannot respect the rules of this house, then it's time for you to go!"

Brian was so angry, spit was flying everywhere as his index finger poked in her general direction. Having made his grand gesture, he folded his arms across his chest and waited.

Connie nodded. "Okay, Brian. I understand." Surprisingly, she was okay with it. Being asked to leave the only home she'd ever known, and she could only assume breaking the bond with her closest relative in such an adversarial way could've— no, would've—shattered the old Connie.

But somehow knowing that shortly she would be back in Michael's arms, where he would soothe her hurt and kiss away her pain, not only made the situation bearable, but somehow had made her unbreakable.

She turned to leave, but apparently Brian was not finished. "If Mom and Dad could see what a little tramp you've become, they would turn over in their graves."

She turned just as she heard Annie's sharply indrawn breath. Glancing at her sister-in-law's hurt expression, Connie felt a rage overcome her. Not because of the insult her brother had hurled at her but because, in doing so, he'd caused Annie even more hurt.

Her eyes narrowed as she faced her brother. "And if they could see what a self-righteous, sanctimonious jackass you've become, they would turn right back over!" She took several quick steps forward, suddenly needing to unburden herself of some of the thoughts she'd carried around inside for too long.

"You know, Brian, I used to look up to you. I used to think you were what every good Christian should be. But you're no Christian. Just a judgmental little man, trying to control things that have nothing to do with you!"

"How dare you talk to me this way!"

"How dare you talk to me this way! I'm as much a full-grown woman as you are a man, and I don't want or need your interference in my life!"

Brian's eyes widened and he stared at her as if she'd simply appeared out of nowhere. Connie understood his confusion. To him, she must seem like someone else. In all the years they'd been siblings, never had she stood up to him, and never had she talked back. Damn, it felt good!

She nodded briskly. "I'll go, Brian. Lord knows, I should've done so years ago. But know this, Brian—I'm done taking instructions from you. I'm done letting you rule my life. Michael is wonderful and I love him, and I fully plan to marry him. And if you can't accept that then as much as I would regret it, I guess I'll have to live without a brother."

Brian closed his eyes, and took a deep fortifying breath, as if regaining control of himself. "Connie, it's not as if I don't want to see you get married and have a family. Of course, I do, but this man—this man took advantage of you!"

Connie took a few more steps toward her brother. Now that he'd calmed down, she was hopeful that they would be able to have a civil conversation about things that should've been said years ago. "No, Brian. Nathan took advantage of me—not, Michael. I know he's your friend and probably will be for many more years, but you have no idea what that man is really like. What he is truly capable of."

She shook her head, trying to sort bad memories from coherent thought. "Michael is exactly who he claims to be. Nathan lied about everything. Everything!" She shrugged, expressing a frustration she'd never come to terms with. "To this day, I don't know why he wanted to marry me. He never wanted me."

Brian was shaking his head. "No! I know you're angry that you couldn't make your marriage work, but I will not hear you slander my friend's good name!"

Connie just stared at her brother, and finally accepted there would be no getting through to him. "Fine, Brian. Have it your way. I'll pack my things and be out of here by this evening."

"What about me, Brian?" Annie's soft voice came out of nowhere, and Connie was unsure of when she'd stood. "Will you hear slander from me?"

Brian turned to his wife with a confused expression on his face. "What are you talking about?"

"I hadn't planned to ever mention it, but Connie's right. You do not know what kind of man Nathan is." She reached up and wiped a tear from her cheek with the back of her hand. "Nathan, I saw him kissing Marla Johnson."

Brian looked back and forth between the two women, his mouth gaping open. Connie was too dumbfounded to say anything. Some part of her mind was not overly surprised, after all that behavior kinda fit right into everything else she knew about her ex-husband. And although she kept it to herself, she knew it wasn't the only time he'd cheated on her.

"It was back when we were first dating," Annie continued, "remember we went to that Christmas party at the Johnsons?"

He shook his head in disbelief. "But, that's impossible! Marla's a married woman, her husband was at that party!"

"And he was a married man, but it didn't stop him," Annie insisted gently. "I saw them together in the pantry. They were too…into what they were doing to notice me." She glanced at Connie apologetically. "I'm sorry, Connie, I didn't say anything. It's just I didn't really know you that well, me and Brian had just started seeing each other. And then, when your marriage ended, I just thought—"

Connie held up a hand to stop her. "It's okay, Annie." She made a small snorting sound. "At least that explains where he was all that time he kept disappearing. I thought he had started smoking again and was sneaking out for smoke breaks."

Her snort turned into a full chuckle as she realized something wonderfully amazing. Hearing about her ex-husband's infidelity didn't hurt. Not even a little bit. It was like listening to the events of someone else's life. She had carried the pain and disappointment of her failed marriage around in her heart for so long, she'd forgotten how it felt to be free of that burden. But, now she was free again and it felt great.

Meanwhile, Brian had placed his hands over his face and was shaking his head in denial. "This is not happening, this is not happening!"

Connie could imagine what he was feeling, discovering that his best friend, his former brother-in-law, was not the man he had thought he was. That instead of being the righteous man of God he had pretended to be with most people, he was in fact, a lying hypocrite…with a mean streak.

Annie cupped his face in her hands. "I'm only telling you now to make you understand that despite what you think, you don't know everything."

"I never claimed to know everything!"

The couple's attention was completely trained on each other and the conversation was sounding more and more like a private one between husband and wife. Connie was wondering if she could creep out of the room without interrupting them.

"Sometimes you do." She lowered her head, and her voice. "Especially when it comes to Connie."

Connie felt a sinking feeling in the pit of her stomach. The last thing she wanted was for the focus of their argument to turn to *her*.

Brian looked at Connie. "I just want what's best for you. You understand that, right?" For a moment, Connie caught of glimpse of the loving brother she had known all her life reflected in his eyes.

"Then trust me to know what's best for me." She lifted her hands in a defeated gesture. "Thirty years of my life are gone, and I have nothing to show for it. I feel like a failure, Brian. I tried to make you happy, and I feel like I even failed at that."

"What are you talking about?" He frowned in genuine confusion.

"I'm thirty years old and I've never even had my own place. I've been married and divorced and only now, for the irst time, am I experiencing love. Real love." She nodded determinedly. "I'm not going to give that up, not even for you."

He rubbed his head, and Connie had no doubt that the women in his life were indeed giving him a headache. "I don't want to take that away from you. I just want you to be decent about it."

Her eyebrow arched in irritation. "Decent? Your kind of decent? Like your good and decent friend, Nath—"

His hand slashed through the air in anger. "Don't worry about Nathan!" His eyes narrowed on some faraway sight. "I'll deal with him later." Absently, Connie watched him take Annie's hand in his. "You should've told me sooner," he muttered.

Annie shrugged in indifference, but Connie could see the relief in her eyes.

"This taking secret trips, getting involved with a strange man… It's just not like you."

Connie laughed, feeling lighter suddenly. "Actually, it's very much like me—the real me. The me Michael loves." She winked at her brother. "You just haven't gotten to know that me, yet. But I hope you'll be willing to."

The brother and sister stood watching each other for several long seconds before he gave a slight nod of agreement. Deciding that they had let out enough skeletons for one afternoon, she turned and headed for her room. "I'm going to pack, I'll say goodbye before I leave."

"I'm sorry," Brian called from behind her. "I lashed out in anger. You don't have to go."

She smiled at her brother, believing for the first time that, maybe in the end, they would remain close. "No, you're right. It's better that I move out. Should've done this a long, long time ago. Only cowardice held me back."

As she reached the doorway, she turned again to the couple still standing by the couch, embraced in a hug. Annie was smiling at her over Brian's shoulder.

"Thank you." Connie mouthed the words.

Only the slightest nod of Annie's head indicated she'd heard.

A short time later, Connie piled the bags and boxes containing most of her personal possessions into the back of her small car and just stood there staring down at it for several moments as it dawned on her that this was the sum of her life until this point.

She had no home of her own, she owned nothing except her car and these things. How had this happened? This was never the life she'd imagined for herself. This was never the plan, but somehow she'd ended up thirty years old living in her brother's spare room.

With a sigh, she closed the trunk and climbed into the driver's seat. With one final glance at the small picturesque home where she'd spent almost her whole life until now, she started the engine and pulled away.

Strangely enough, she wasn't nearly as upset as she would've imagined, given all that had happened that afternoon. Instead, she felt this indefinable sense of excitement swelling up in her. A completely unaccounted for feeling of euphoria.

This wasn't the end of something, it was the beginning. She had no doubt that given time and space, she and Brian would eventually mend any fences that had been torn down between them. But more importantly, now she could begin to live. Really live.

The life she'd always imagined: full of love and passion and freedom. That was it. She felt truly free, more free than she'd ever felt before and it was all because of Michael. His love gave her the courage to express herself as she had never known. He was the only person who really knew her, because he was the only person she'd ever felt free enough with to show her real self to. And like a reflection in a mirror, she was able to see herself through his eyes…and she loved what she saw there. She loved the way she felt with him, the way she was with him, and most of all she loved him. And she had every intention of spending the rest of her life showing him just how much his love meant to her.

A blob of water hit her windshield, followed by another and then another and before long, it was coming down in a steady stream. She turned on the wipers and smiled to herself, cracked the window and took a deep breath.

She had always loved the way it smelled when it rained. She took another deep breath and sighed in satisfaction. For the first time in a long time, she felt like she could breathe.

After Connie left, Michael had spent the rest of the afternoon at home reviewing the blueprints for a new plane design. He'd become so engrossed in reading and making notes on the various components that hours passed without him realizing it.

When his cell phone rang, it startled him and he glanced up at the clock and then out the window of his penthouse. The sun was just beginning to set, and at some point it had started raining.

He reached across the table and grabbed his phone. "Hello?"

"Hi, I'm downstairs and need your help with my bags."

Michael sat straight up in his chair. "Your bags? Does this mean…?"

"For now—can you come help me?"

"Did you go see your brother? What'd he say?"

"Long story."

"What happened?"

"He kicked me out."

"What?"

"Michael, this conversation would be much better sitting

on your couch sipping a glass of wine. Instead of standing in the pouring rain."

"Sorry, I'll be right down."

Forty-five minutes later, her bags were stacked high on the floor of the master suite, and they were indeed snuggled up together on the couch, sipping red wine.

Michael kissed the top of her head where it was nestled beneath his chin. "Okay, start at the beginning."

Connie sighed in contentment, truly not wanting to ruin the perfect moment rehashing the argument with her brother. "Not much to tell. He asked me to move and I agreed. Although, in all fairness, he did take it back in the end. But I decided my moving out wasn't such a bad idea after all. And so, here I am."

"Well, since I got a sexy new roommate out of the bargain, I shouldn't complain. But the idea of him throwing you out makes me want to go over there and beat his ass."

"I told you he took it back in the end."

"Still…"

"Shh." She reached up and gave him a quick kiss. "I'm happy. Don't mess it up."

Michael smiled. "Your wish is my command."

They lay on the couch in quiet contentment for several minutes. Connie was sorting through all the ways she had changed since meeting Michael, but then decided she hadn't actually changed. No, being with Michael had simply allowed her to be herself. And since she'd never felt free enough to be herself before, that self seemed somehow different, somehow changed. When in fact she had been there all along, buried deep inside her miserable fake self. And the courage to fulfill one of her dreams had led her to the man who would fulfill all of her dreams. But despite all that, there was still more to be uncovered, more self to be discovered.

"Michael?"

"Hmm."

"I want you to know, my living here, this is temporary."

He shifted his body so he could look directly at her, a small frown creased his brow. "What are you saying?"

"I think I want to get my own place."

"Why? There is plenty of room here. More than enough."

She sat up, and took a deep breath. "I know. It's just I want to try living on my own for a while."

Michael opened his mouth to argue and closed it suddenly. He stared into her eyes for several long moments before a small smile came across his face.

"All right." He nodded and returned to his comfortable position. "Okay, get your own place, I understand."

As she settled back against his chest once more, Connie smiled to herself knowing that he did. Because he understood *her,* better than anyone ever had.

She yawned, feeling warm and contented, and realized she was slowly dozing off to sleep when Michael spoke from over her head.

"Connie?"

"Yes?"

"I know you said you don't want to rush into marriage, but how about you say yes now, and we just have a really long engagement?"

Connie laughed. "How long are we talking?"

She felt him shrug around her. "As long as you want, or need." He kissed her on the top of her head again. "I just want to get you off the dance floor before some other man grabs your attention."

She grinned up at him. "You don't have to worry about anyone else grabbing my attention. You have no competition."

"So you think." He huffed. "That's because you don't know what you look like when you dance."

She chuckled, silently wondering at the miracle that had caused their lives to intersect.

"Well?" he asked when she did not answer the question.

"Well…what?" she teased.

"Don't play coy. Will you marry me…eventually?"

She turned and wrapped her arms around his neck. "Yes my beautiful island lover. Yes."

* * * * *

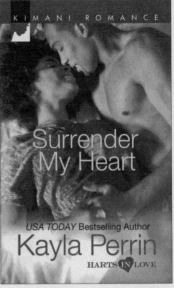

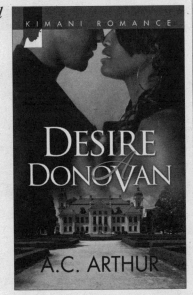